WHEN WE MEET AGAIN

JILL STEEPLES

Boldwood

First published in Great Britain in 2022 by Boldwood Books Ltd.

Copyright © Jill Steeples, 2022

Cover Design by Debbie Clement Design

Cover Photography: Shutterstock

Every effort has been made to obtain the necessary permissions with reference to copyright material, both illustrative and quoted. We apologise for any omissions in this respect and will be pleased to make the appropriate acknowledgements in any future edition.

A CIP catalogue record for this book is available from the British Library.

Paperback ISBN 978-1-80280-742-4

Large Print ISBN 978-1-80280-743-1

Hardback ISBN 978-1-80280-741-7

Ebook ISBN 978-1-80280-744-8

Kindle ISBN 978-1-80280-745-5

Audio CD ISBN 978-1-80280-736-3

MP3 CD ISBN 978-1-80280-737-0

Digital audio download ISBN 978-1-80280-740-0

Boldwood Books Ltd
23 Bowerdean Street
London SW6 3TN
www.boldwoodbooks.com

For Nick, Tom and Ellie

1

I'm not superstitious. Not really. I mean, I wouldn't walk underneath a ladder or anything like that, because that would be silly. And if I see a magpie, then naturally I'd do a little scout around the area to see if I can find his mate and if not, I'll chirp, 'Good morning, Mr Magpie, how are you and your family today?' but that's just normal stuff. The sort of thing everyone does, right? And it wasn't as if Friday 13 held any trepidation for me whatsoever because it's just a day like any other day. Or at least I thought it was. That was until that strange afternoon. The afternoon of Friday 13 April when the events unfolded that were to change my life forever.

* * *

'You still here?' Damon Mitchell was standing in the doorway to my office, bouncing a ball casually on the floor, his usual sharp suit replaced with white three-quarter-length shorts and a low-slung vest, showing off muscles I hadn't known he possessed. The sight on a Friday afternoon was disconcerting in the extreme and I glanced away, feeling colour tinge my cheeks, before sneaking another look.

'Almost done,' I said breezily, picking up the management reports from my desk and popping them in the drawer below, locking the cabinet with my key.

When I looked up, Damon was bent over, stretching his hamstrings, looking up at me from beneath his floppy fringe. Did he really have to do that in my office?

'We're still a player short, Alice. Why don't you come along? You never know, you might enjoy yourself.'

'Ha, believe me, I know,' I laughed. I had no desire to be getting hot and sweaty in front of Damon.

No, retaining a dignified distance at all times was definitely the way to go with ace sportsmen like Damon. I pushed my chair beneath my desk before reaching for my jacket from the coat stand. 'Ball games are not my thing. But you have a great time. You can tell me all about it on Monday.'

'Ah, well, at least I tried. You have a good weekend, Alice.'

'Yeah, you too, Damon.'

It wasn't just that I'm not the athletic type without any competitive spirit whatsoever. As PA to Simon Ibottson, CEO of Merron Enterprises, I'd always stayed a respectful distance away from the chummy camaraderie that existed on the sales, marketing and finance floors. I couldn't really be seen to be indulging in the late-night drinking sessions, even if I'd wanted to. Instead, I tried to hold onto a professional and friendly demeanour at all times.

''Night, Alice!' Damon called.

Outside, still smiling, I climbed into my car, deciding because of the uncharacteristically warm weather to pull down the lid. The first time that year. It was one of those glorious spring days that tantalises with the promise of summer, and the prospect of a whole weekend ahead with nothing to do was bliss. I ran my hands through my hair, feeling the week's stresses melt away. A couple of glossy magazines, a pile of soppy rom-com DVDs, a box of tissues, a family bag of Maltesers and a couple of bottles of Sauvignon Blanc. There, my weekend was now satisfyingly chock-a-block.

I took the back roads home, a journey I could have done with my eyes shut, although even in my carefree state, I was sensible enough to realise that probably wasn't the best idea. I loved that drive, my eyes always picking out something new along the country lanes that wound their way through the villages. The picturesque backdrop of green tended fields, stone buildings and colourful bulbs popping their heads up, greeting the lengthening days, only heightened my sense of wellbeing. With the music turned up high, the wind blowing through my hair, I tapped my fingers on the steering wheel, singing along to the Red Hot Chili Peppers.

It was only as I rounded the sharp bend before the road opened up into beckoning countryside that I became aware of something. Something odd.

A sense of dread rose in my chest. Where was everyone? It was a Friday afternoon and there wasn't a soul around. Despite me being buffeted by the wind, there was a noticeable stillness that lent an eerie quality to the surroundings.

Shivering, I drove on and that's when my foot took on a life force of its own, involuntarily slamming down onto the brake as I wrestled with the steering wheel, guiding the car into a small cutaway at the side of a large field. My breath quickening, I climbed out and, standing on tiptoes, gazed over the hedgerow at the scene in front of me. It took my breath away. I hadn't imagined it after all. A car – silver, large – was upended, its wheels still spinning, the side panels crushed, its windows shattered. On the ground twenty feet away from the car was a solitary figure, crumpled on the grass.

No, no, no!

I don't do blood or infirmity or disaster. Frantically, I looked around, desperate for someone to join me, preferably a paramedic type, but there wasn't a soul in sight. It was up to me to go over, but my feet felt welded to the ground. Surely no one could have crawled out of that car alive. Reaching inside my jacket for my mobile, I started to walk, before quickly breaking into a run, looking ahead and trying at the same time to find my phone. Damn! Where was the bloody thing?

Within moments, I was beside the wreckage and almost wept with relief to find that the bundle on the ground was in fact a man, alive and, if not exactly kicking, looking remarkably un-scathed, as he sat there, his arms hugging his knees.

'Thank God,' I gasped, 'are you all right?' I bent down to meet his eyes, my hand reaching out to touch his shoulder as if to check he was in one piece.

'Hi.' He smiled lightly, his piercing grey eyes latching onto mine, holding me entranced. He ran a hand through mussed-up black hair, before ex-tending his arm in friendly greeting as if we'd just been introduced at some social occasion.

'My phone!' I needed my bloody phone. 'I think I've left it in my car.' Don't panic, I screeched in-wardly, my arms waving frantically towards the main road. 'I'll just run and fetch it, ring for an am-bulance.'

'No! Don't.' He spoke with an authority that stopped me in mid-flight.

'But you need to be checked over. You look, um...' Awful. He looked worse than awful, but in such a beguiling way that I couldn't drag my eyes away from him. His warm voice was gently hypnotic, too. Weirdly, it was like reconnecting with a long-lost friend. 'A bit peaky to me,' I managed, my hands reaching out to touch his face. 'You're probably in shock.'

He emitted a hollow laugh.

'Shock? Yeah, I am a bit.' He shook his head, bemused. 'But really, I'm okay.' His expression softened. 'Besides, the emergency services, they've been.'

'What? And just left you here? No. They wouldn't do that.'

'No.' He eased himself up to a standing position, his long body uncurling. He must have been six foot two at least, the muscles in his upper arms and shoulders clearly defined beneath his creased blue shirt. 'The accident happened earlier. The police and ambulance came and sorted everything. It's fine. All fine.' He brushed himself

down distractedly. 'They gave me the all-clear.
There's nothing to worry about. I just came back
to have a look. To see what happened.' He let out
a long slow whistle. 'Can't believe the state of the
car.'

'Me neither.' I turned to look at the mangled
mess. The accident had happened earlier? I felt certain I'd missed it by only a matter of minutes. I
must have imagined those wheels spinning. Still,
this guy looked pretty shaken up. And what was he
thinking, coming back to examine the wreckage?
He couldn't just hang around here in the middle of
a field, reliving the awful incident in his mind. A
light wind was whipping across the hedges,
taunting my goosebumps. It wouldn't do him any
good to be stuck in the freezing cold after the
trauma he'd just been through. One thing was for
certain, though, his car wasn't going anywhere but
the salvage yard.

'Is someone coming to pick you up?'

He tilted his head, looking puzzled.

'They'll have to take the car away. Examine it, I
guess.' His hand caressed the misshapen metal of
the bonnet.

'No, I meant you, is someone coming to collect you? To take you home?'

'I don't know.' He gave a funny little laugh. 'I don't think so.'

Really, it was shocking, the way the country was going. This guy was clearly in a bad way. Okay, so he had no broken bones, but anyone with an inch of compassion could tell that he was in deep shock. His dark eyes were hollow, his skin tinged with grey and the hairs on his arms were standing on end. What were the emergency services thinking, leaving the poor man in this condition? He should be in hospital being checked over, or at least at home, tucked up in bed.

'Look, come with me,' I said, offering my arm. 'Let's go to my car and then we'll decide what to do.'

'Will you take me home?' he asked, his voice lifting.

'Of course I will.' I patted his arm gently, the touch of his skin under my fingers sending an icy chill down my bones. 'Gosh, you're freezing. Come on, I've got a blanket in the car. Do you think I should ring someone? Tell them what's happened, that you're okay?'

'No, there's no one,' he said, matter-of-factly. 'I, um,' he faltered, shaking his head again as if trying to make sense of it all, putting on a brave face for my benefit. My heart tugged at his vulnerability. 'Could we go to yours, maybe?' he added.

His imploring gaze touched me deep inside. I didn't know why, but for whatever reason, he couldn't face going home yet. For the moment, it seemed he wanted only the comfort of a stranger.

'Yes, yes, of course.' We walked together away from the crash scene, me hanging onto his arm, un-sure whether I was supporting him or he was holding me up. 'I only live down the road. I think we could both do with a nice cup of tea. Then we can think about having you looked over, seeing a doctor or something.'

'Tea sounds good,' he said, in barely more than a whisper.

It wasn't until I'd put him in the passenger seat and tucked a blanket around his frozen limbs, then pulled closed the lid of the car, that the second re-ally freaky thing of the day occurred to me. Ma-noeuvring the car out of the layby, I glanced across at the man whose name I didn't know yet with a stirring of recognition. And then I looked at him again, examining the defined jawline, the set of his mouth which made him look as though he was permanently smiling, and the deep-set grey eyes, which when they focused on you made you feel that you were at the centre of his universe.

It was the eyes that were the clincher. Intense and magnetic, they'd held my gaze on many an occasion. With a jolt of recognition, I gasped. James McArthur, Mr Daytime Television himself, affectionately known as Jimmy Mack to his adoring public, was sitting in my car. The realisation turned me into a gibbering, quivering wreck. Oh, my gawd!

His black hair, usually worn short and neat on screen, had grown longer and swept over one eye, giving him a mysterious air. Wayward tendrils skimmed the edge of his collar and I had to suppress an urge to lean over and tidy them up with my fingers.

He was even more gorgeous in the flesh than on screen, if that was possible, and my breath caught at the back of my throat as my pulse went into overdrive. Being a master in stating the bleeding obvious, I said, ever-so-not-so-casually, 'You're Jimmy

Mack, aren't you? Off the telly?' Talk about losing all coolness and credibility in the space of a few seconds.

He turned his gaze on me, smiled a megawatt smile that sent my insides to mush, and nodded.

'What's your name, then?' he asked, as if it had only just occurred to him that I might have one.

'Alice. Alice Fletcher.' Now it was me shaking my head. I couldn't help imagining what everyone would say when I told them I'd acted as a guardian angel to probably the most recognisable man in the public eye and we were planning on sharing a cup of tea together. How amazing was that? Maybe I'd even get to appear on his show. 'Meet Alice Fletcher, the heroine who rescued our very own Jimmy Mack from his car wreckage.' That was exactly the sort of sensationalism his show went in for.

Back at my flat, in a flurry of heightened excitement, I clucked around him like a mother hen. I made a cup of tea, put him on the sofa, threw a duvet over him and generally kept an eye on my unexpected visitor. I was desperate to contact someone, anyone, to let them know what had happened, but he wasn't having any of it. Maybe he was on his way to somewhere he shouldn't have been, I mused, wondering about the private side to this very public man.

Probably, once he'd had a rallying cup of tea, gathered his thoughts a little, I'd be able to get more sense out of him, but for the time being, he wasn't the most forthcoming of house guests.

'I think I might just close my eyes for a moment.' He put down his empty mug on the wicker coffee table and settled back in his seat, stretching his arms above his head. 'Is that okay?'

'Yes, you go ahead. I've got plenty to be getting on with here. Just give me a shout if you need anything.'

A little thrill of excitement ran through me. Was Jimmy Mack really sitting on my sofa? Or was I part of some elaborate TV prank? He looked real enough to me. As his eyes flickered shut, I studied his familiar features more closely. The contours of his face, the strong turn of his jaw, the wide lips smiling even in rest; it was like looking at a member of my family. Weirdly, it seemed perfectly natural that he should be sitting there.

But then again...

What if something happened to him?

A ripple of unease rose in my throat. What if he fell into some sort of delayed coma? Or contracted hypothermia, ending up dead in my living room? That would take some explaining. Before I'd even had the chance to grab a couple of autographs off him as well. Desperation bubbled up in me. Celebrity or not, I had to get him out of my flat ASAP so that the responsibility of looking after the nation's favourite presenter could be offloaded onto someone else.

For the moment, though, he wasn't going anywhere. He looked right at home on my squidgy sofa, his head resting on his arm. I supposed it was only natural he'd want to sleep after the ordeal he'd been through. It seemed a shame to wake him, so instead I wandered into the kitchen, placing the dirty cups into the dishwasher. I threw some clothes into the washing machine. Skimmed the pile of paperwork waiting patiently on the side. Checked my emails. Then I read my horoscope in the local newspaper:

A chance encounter could bring unexpected results. Keep an open mind and go with the flow, you never know where it might lead you!

I laughed out loud. There wasn't much else I could do in the circumstances.

No, all I could do was wait. I drummed my fingertips on the worktop, frequently gazing over at my guest, looking for any signs of life. And then I waited some more.

At eight o'clock, with no sign of my visitor rousing, I made another cup of tea and a lot more noise in the process. I flung open cupboard doors, banged mugs down on the surfaces and hummed loudly. It was no good – a more direct approach was required.

'Jimmy?' I leant over him, whispering in his ear. A musky, earthy scent reached my nostrils. 'Jimmy,' I said, gently shaking his shoulder, 'would you like another cup of tea?'

He murmured something unintelligible which, after that amount of time, was an almighty relief, I have to say.

'Good,' I said sharply. 'Then perhaps you'd like

something to eat. Might make you feel a bit better.'
Then perhaps you'll vacate my sofa and leave me
alone to my weekend of domestic bliss, I kept to
myself. 'I'll put the telly on, shall I? We can catch
the news.'

I zapped the remote at the telly, popped into the
kitchen to fetch the mugs of tea and came back into
the living room. That's when I received the third
and most spectacularly freaky shock of the day. So
much so that I screamed, dropping the mugs to the
floor, the contents spraying my cream leather sofa
and gardenia walls. That woke him, once and
for all.

'Jesus Christ! What is it?' He leapt up from the
sofa, only just escaping the hot liquid, and looked
at me accusingly.

'You. It's you.' I looked from him to the screen.
'On the telly.' I pointed at the box in the corner of
the room for good measure just in case he had any
doubt as to what I was freaking out about.

We were standing a hair's breadth away from
each other and I felt a surge of emotion rise
within me, the air in the room suddenly
electrified.

'You!' I repeated, my mouth gaping open like a befuddled goldfish.

'Ah... yes,' he said, having the grace to look a little sheepish, 'perhaps I should have mentioned it.'

I sank down onto the sofa in the place recently vacated by Jimmy, my head falling into my hands. Maybe there'd been some kind of mistake.

'You're... you're...' I gulped. No, it couldn't be. 'You're... dead?' I faltered, looking up into his eyes, which seemed so much greyer and deeper than before.

He shrugged, an apologetic smile forming on his lips.

'Yep, I am.'

No mistake, then.

* * *

Millions of people were in mourning following the tragic death of one of the country's most well-known and well-loved celebrities in a freak accident. Grim-faced newsreaders repeated the news of the untimely demise of Mr Nice Guy, raking over the details of his last hours to find answers to the most unfathomable question. How exactly had Jimmy Mack died? Why had it happened? What private demons had driven Jimmy Mack to an early grave?

In the surreal surroundings of my flat, which had taken on an otherworldly quality with the presence of Jimmy lounging on my sofa, the television confirmed to me what I really didn't want to believe. I was now wrapped up under the duvet, having nabbed it back from Jimmy, considering my need to be much greater than his. Hardly daring to surface, only my eyes peeped over the top of the cover at the screen, as tears rolled down my cheeks for the dead man standing beside me.

'Please don't cry!' he said, pacing up and down and flapping his arms ineffectively.

'Don't cry? Are you serious?' I jumped up from the sofa and followed him step for step across the carpet. 'You are... a hugely famous TV star and you're standing in my living room and if that wasn't mind-blowing enough... you're also... you're also dead! How do you expect me to react?'

'Yeah, well, if it's any consolation, it's pretty

weird for me too. Do you think I wanted to end up here? I should be on my way to the Heavenly Hilton or wherever it is you're supposed to go, escorted by a couple of blonde angels.'

'This is crazy!' I cried, attempting to hurl the duvet across the room, but only managing to tangle it between my legs. 'Let's just get this clear,' I added, slowing my breathing, 'you are actually... a ghost, then?'

'Well, it looks that way.' He actually laughed. As if this were a laughing matter. He glanced down at his moleskin trousers, the pale blue chambray shirt; his sleeves rolled to his elbows, with not even the tiniest speck of blood in sight. He looked real enough to me, solid, living, eminently touchable.

'No!' I shook my head in denial. 'I just can't get my head around this at all.'

I grabbed a handful of tissues from the box on the table and blew my nose noisily, looking at Jimmy accusingly. What the hell were we supposed to do now? Who should I call? The police, the doctor, an undertaker?

I took a deep breath.

'So, um, tell me. How did it happen then? The accident?'

'Well, that's the funny thing, I don't really know. It all happened so quickly. I was on my way to my parents' place in Mettlesham. It's their ruby wedding anniversary this weekend and I was supposed to be taking them out to dinner tonight to celebrate.' He screwed up his mouth, looking wistful. 'I left the studio early afternoon and, as it was such a beautiful day, I decided to take the back roads instead of using the motorway.' He paused as if reliving those last few moments. 'I came round the bend and then, well, the steering just flew out of my hands. There was nothing I could do. The car flipped over and over. I didn't think it was going to stop. And then my head hit the steering wheel or the dashboard, I can't remember which. And that was it. Game over.'

My gaze settled on the innocuous-looking graze adorning his forehead.

'Did it hurt?' I didn't really want to know the answer but couldn't stop myself from asking.

'Not really.' He shrugged, pondering the question. 'It was pretty instantaneous. There was a lot of noise. In my head. And lights, lots of flashing lights, but I didn't really feel anything.'

'No? Well, that's something, I suppose.' I sighed. 'I am so sorry,' I said, sinking back down onto the sofa, not knowing what else to say. What exactly do you say to a dead man? The thought of his grieving family, friends and whole legion of fans was uppermost in my mind.

'Don't worry about it. It's hardly your fault. I appreciate this must be very strange for you, me being here, but please don't cry over me. The whole dying thing... it's not half as bad as you'd imagine.'

I felt like sticking my fingers in my ears and la-la-ing into oblivion, but Jimmy was looking at me intently.

'Well, you're looking better than when I first came across you, I must admit.' A bit peaky still, but his voice sounded much stronger and his presence seemingly so much more vivid.

'Hey, I bet I'm the best-looking dead man you've ever met?'

I couldn't argue with that. He was the best-looking man I'd ever met. Living or otherwise.

When he laughed, his grey eyes twinkled mis-

chievously, but I was finding it hard to find anything to laugh about. This whole episode was
making me feel very uneasy.

Jimmy went on, considering me thoughtfully.
'It's just that I think there may have been a few
problems in the, um, well, I don't know what you'd
call it, but in the handing over process, I suppose.'

'The handing over process?' A feeling of trepidation filled every pore in my body. 'What do you
mean, exactly?' I asked, not certain I wanted to hear
the answer.

He scratched his head, managing to look both
vulnerable and gorgeous in equal measure. 'For
some reason, I seem to have got stuck here with
you. Obviously not alive, but not fully gone over to
the other side either. Betwixt and between, I suppose. I think that's why you were sent my way. To
help me.'

'Ha, ha!' I laughed, rather too heartily, only now
it was Jimmy's turn to look serious. 'But how can I
possibly help you?' I said slowly, quietly, the deep
apprehension growing in my chest.

'To get to the other side, of course.' He said it as
if it were the most natural thing in the world.

2

Why me? It was a question I asked myself a dozen times over in the hours following Jimmy's arrival in my life.

I liked to pride myself on my efficiency and capability. It's what I'm good at. Throw a problem my way and I'll sort it. Even if I don't immediately know the answer, I'll find someone who does. But whoever it was up there who thought my organisational skills stretched to finding homes for recently deceased people, however well known and however gorgeous, was surely having a joke at my expense.

I tried to broach this sensitive subject with Jimmy.

'Were you not given any idea when you, um, passed... what you were supposed to do? Where you were meant to go?'

In a short space of time, he seemed to have made himself very comfy on my sofa and was brandishing the remote control with authority, flicking between channels to get the most up-to-date coverage on his demise.

'Huh?' He looked mildly irritated as he turned his gaze to look at me.

'When you... you know...' I didn't like to say the word aloud, almost as if I didn't mention it then it wouldn't be such a permanent arrangement. Instead, I made a genteel fainting motion.

'Pegged it, you mean? Nope. There was no welcoming committee or induction manual, not even a map pointing me in the direction of the upwards escalator or the downward one.'

He didn't look unduly concerned about the whole episode – he was much more interested in what was happening on the telly.

'Would you look at him?' He was sitting on the edge of his chair, leaning forward, jabbing his finger at the screen. 'I don't believe it!'

It was Barney Roberts, the young and dynamic presenter of *Win, Win, Win!*, the daily quiz show, his usual cheeky-chappie persona replaced with a sombre mask.

'We are all deeply shocked and saddened by the untimely death of Jimmy Mack, a much-loved and respected colleague here at Studio 99. Our thoughts and condolences go out to his family at this very sad time.'

'Jeez! What a bloody hypocrite! How he's got the nerve to stand there saying he'll miss my friendship and my support, as though we were best buddies, I really don't know. The guy's always hated me.'

Secretly I was a bit of a fan of Barney Roberts. Much more of a fan than I'd ever been of Jimmy Mack, but now wasn't the time to mention it.

'Don't be like that,' I said, crouching down to look Jimmy in the eye, picking up his hand. I didn't want to appear rude, but I couldn't help myself from staring at his features. They were all so famil-iar, all so real. My thumb stroked the length of his long fingers. How could he possibly be a ghost when he looked and felt so normal? A shiver tormented my spine as my gaze drifted between Jimmy and the TV screen.

'He looks genuinely upset, everyone is, you can see that, surely?' I did my best to reassure him. 'It's such a shock for us all.'

'Don't you believe a word of it. It's all an act, he's just milking the moment. He'll be plotting to take over my daytime show already. You mark my words. As soon as he's off air, he'll be in discussions with the studio bosses.'

'Do you think?' I asked, not really believing him. Obviously he was distressed. Who wouldn't be in the circumstances? I took a deep breath and tried to find the right words. 'Well, try not to upset yourself over it. It's not as though you can do anything about it now. Now that you're, um, dead...'

I flinched under the dagger-like stare from Jimmy, realising I'd failed on the comforting words front. 'And it's not as though anyone could ever really take over your slot,' I added, quickly. 'There'll only ever be one Jimmy Mack. I mean, who could ever replace you?'

He sighed, stretching his arms up above his head, looking marginally appeased. I was beginning to realise that Jimmy had an ego to match his huge talent.

'Hmm, I suppose you're right.'

'Of course I am.' I patted his hand again, in a move that was becoming second nature to me. 'More urgently, though, we need to work out what we're going to do about... um, moving you on. Getting you to the right place. You won't want to be hanging around here for any length of time.'

Jimmy shrugged, unconcerned, looking as if it wouldn't actually be the worst thing in the world.

'Don't worry,' he said. 'I'm sure it's just a minor hiccup. When you think about it, the amount of through traffic being handled on a daily basis, this sort of thing is bound to happen occasionally. I'll probably be moved on in a day or two.'

A day or two? I was hoping for an hour at the most. Much more of this and my nerves would be frazzled to pieces.

I sighed, taking the remote control from Jimmy's hold and switching off the telly.

'Hey, what did you do that for?'

'Well, it can't do you any good seeing all that stuff. It must be very upsetting, knowing you're leaving all your friends and family behind. Seeing them so distraught, too. It isn't helping anyone. Your parents...'

Tears rushed to my eyes and I blinked them away. What had Jimmy done to be landed with me, a simpering blubbering mess? I simply couldn't bear it. To think of his poor mum and dad waiting expectantly at home for their son to arrive for what should have been a celebratory event, only to receive instead the most unwelcome visitor on their doorstep, a police officer bearing bad news. It was too much to contemplate.

'Hey.' He jumped up and wrapped his arms around me. I sighed, his embrace feeling strange but oddly comforting, the very tips of my fingers and toes tingling in expectation. I couldn't remember the last time a man held me that way. He pulled back, holding my face captive in his hands, his look beseeching.

'Don't cry. Not for me.' I took a deep breath, taking in his earthy masculine scent, his face dangerously close to mine. 'I'm here, aren't I?' He pulled away, holding out his arms wide. 'Not exactly in the peak of health, admittedly, but I'm here.'

When he laughed, his deep grey eyes twinkled like stars in the night sky. It went a small way to making me feel better.

'Yes, but, it's so sad...' Now, I couldn't stop the big gulping sobs that had been bubbling in my chest from erupting.

'No, not really. It's kind of hard to explain, but it all feels perfectly natural when it happens to you. As if it's the right thing at the right time. Do you know what I mean? I've always believed that things happen for a reason, and this just proves it! Sure, it's tough for the people left behind, but it's something they'll work through. And really, if you've ever held anyone close to your heart, you know that you'll never completely leave them behind just because you die. I'll get together again with them all one day, you can bet your life on it.'

I screwed my face up, wincing at his choice of words.

'Sorry,' he held up his hands, 'not the best turn of phrase. But really, it's no big deal.'

No big deal? It was the biggest thing that had

ever happened in my life. And I hadn't even known Jimmy before he died. My whole body trembled with shock and terror.

'But what about your mum and dad? Your friends? Was there anyone special?' I asked, my mind rushing in each and every direction.

He dropped his head to one side, giving me a quizzical look.

'A girlfriend?' I said tentatively. I was pretty certain he wasn't gay, although now, as he observed me thoughtfully, I wondered for the briefest moment if I'd got him all wrong.

'Nope, there isn't anyone, no one special, at least.' He looked wistful for a moment. 'Mum and Dad,' he stuttered, 'they'll find this hard, but they will get through it. They're very strong together and they have lots of support around them. They'll be okay. In time.'

Sadness washed over me. There was nothing I could do for him, nor for his loved ones who were left behind. I felt totally helpless. Jimmy was putting on a good show of coping, but his under-lying vulnerability was tangible. There must be something I could do to help. Restlessness made me itchy.

'Well, we can't just sit around here waiting for the ghost train to turn up. We have to do something. Find out how we can get you sent on your way to your rightful place in the... in the, um, universe.'

'Great! And you have some ideas on how we might do that, then?'

'No, not yet. But how difficult can it be?'

Jimmy shrugged, his dark eyebrows shooting high up into his forehead.

'Tomorrow, we'll get started,' I said, sounding much more confident than I felt. 'We'll do some research, there must be oodles of stuff on the internet about it.'

'Yeah, I bet,' said Jimmy doubtfully. 'There is one thing you could do for me before then, though.'

'Yes, of course.'

'Do you have anything to eat?'

'You're hungry?' I asked, my lip curling involuntarily in disbelief.

'Are you kidding? I'm bloody ravenous. I've had a heavy day out there.'

My mind did a quick inventory of the contents of my larder. I hadn't been food shopping in days, but I knew there was a loaf of bread and some bacon in the fridge.

'How does a bacon sandwich sound?'

'Heavenly!' he sighed with an enormous grin.

A ghost with a sense of humour, a possessive regard of my remote control and a healthy appetite, sitting large as life in my living room, was something that might take a bit of getting used to, but I supposed sharing a bacon sarnie and a cup of tea would be a good place to start.

3

The doorbell reverberated through my flat early the next morning. I jumped out of bed, panic washing over me. The events of yesterday afternoon and evening flashed into my head in a messy jumble. It was a dream, right? I'd imagined the whole thing. Thank goodness for that. Poking my head out of the bedroom door, I saw the remains of our late-night snack. Two empty plates, two empty mugs and the faint whiff of bacon lingering in the air. Definitely not a dream. Maybe some sort of mental break-down then, I thought, with just a faint edge of hope. Even that scenario seemed preferable to the reality creeping into my mind like the early morning sunshine filtering into the hallway. I tiptoed down the corridor and stopped outside the guest bedroom, gently pushing open the door, hoping against hope that it would be empty. There, sprawled over the double bed, his long limbs tangled in the white sheets, was the new man in my life, Jimmy Mack. No dream, but a living nightmare.

The doorbell rang again, more insistently this time.

'Coming,' I called hastily, trying to rid myself of the overwhelming sense of guilt I felt. Okay, so there was a dead man in my flat, but it wasn't as if I was personally responsible or anything like that.

'About time.' Lexie grinned, holding open her arms for our customary hug, as she stood in the doorway. Purple tufts of wayward hair framed her elfin features. A multicoloured stripy short skirt, mauve leggings and black T-shirt completed her inimitable look.

'What kept you?' she asked, as she swept past me. 'Didn't get you out of bed, did I?'

'It's the weekend,' I muttered. Lexie would be onto all of this in a matter of minutes. 'It's allowed!'

'Really,' she said slowly, inflecting that one word

with a whole lot of meaning. Her eyes were wide as she marched around my flat like a police officer on a raid, scanning the remains of last night's impromptu supper party. 'I haven't interrupted anything here, have I?'

'Don't be ridiculous,' I said, a little too defensively. 'Sarah popped round last night, that's all. It was late by the time she left. I just didn't get round to cleaning up.'

'Sarah, eh? Do I know her?' That familiar impish grin rested on her lips as she looked at me through narrowed eyes and then she took off, running down my hallway and flinging open my bedroom door.

'Hey! What are you doing?' Silly question really because I knew exactly what she was doing, searching for some mystery man hiding in my bedroom. If only it was as simple as that.

'Just checking,' she said, eyeing me suspiciously. She emerged from my room and her gaze settled on the closed guest room door, before her eyes darted across to mine and then back to the shut door. She hesitated for a moment before dashing to open it.

'No, don't!' I screamed, but it was too late. With

my heart in my mouth, I watched as Lexie surveyed the contents of my spare room. I squeezed my eyes tight and held my breath.

'Disappointing as ever, Alice,' she sighed, a look of contempt on her face. 'I must admit, though, you had me going there for a moment. I really thought I might find some hunk hiding beneath the bed for once.'

My breathing steadied for a moment.

'If I had anyone in my flat, why on earth would I be hiding him away?' I said, feeling only slightly aggrieved that the idea of a man being in my bedroom was so outrageous. The commotion must have woken Jimmy, surely? Hopefully he'd done the sensible thing and made himself scarce. Mind you, thinking about it, there wasn't a whole host of hiding places in that room, just the bed, a small cupboard and a pile of ironing overflowing from a wicker chair. I was pretty certain he couldn't be lurking under there. Perhaps he was performing some spectral hanging-out-of-the-window manoeuvre.

'Hmm, I suppose,' said Lexie, her interest evaporating. She wandered off in the direction of the kitchen. 'I'll stick the kettle on, shall I? I'm dying for a coffee.'

'Um, yeah, great,' I said, taking up the spot just vacated by my sister, realising Jimmy hadn't performed any disappearing act at all. He was still there on the bed where I'd last seen him, all 6'2" tanned, toned inches of him, completely comatose. I could even detect the slightest hint of a snore coming from out of his mouth. At that precise moment, he rolled over, displaying a very decent torso and much more in the process.

Jimmy Mack, recently deceased, was as large as life in my bedroom, seemingly apparent only to me. What on earth was I going to do with him? Apart from watch over him all day, which at that moment didn't seem such a bad idea. The bacon sandwich and a restorative night's sleep had clearly done him the power of good; his skin now radiated an almost healthy glow, the washed-out grey look of yesterday thankfully gone.

Quietly, I pulled the door shut, breathing quickly, hoping against hope that when I came to open it again, my visiting ghost would have decided to take up residence elsewhere.

'So I thought we'd go down to the village and do some shopping,' Lexie called. 'I'm on the lookout for a cape, something goth-ish. I'm sure they'll have something on the market.'

Glad of the distraction, I followed her into the kitchen.

'Great,' I said, thinking some fresh air might give me some much-needed thinking space, time in which to decide what to do with Jimmy Mack. 'Although I can't be long. I have some work to do.'

'At the weekend? I hope they're paying you overtime.'

'It's just some loose ends I need to tie up. You know me, I don't like leaving any jobs unfinished.'

But it wasn't work that was troubling me so much as what to do about my unexpected house guest. Mentally I'd drawn up a plan of action.

Check my junk folder – maybe there was an email with the very important instructions I was missing.

Google 'ghosts and how to get rid of them'.

And then I was stumped. Check Tripadvisor for heavenly resorts?

Aargh, it was hopeless.

At work, I was used to things being thrown at me. Could I organise an eleventh-hour meeting with executives from three different continents? No problem.

Book the flights, find hotels, arrange conferences? Leave it with me.

Field my boss's telephone calls, emails and unplanned personal visits? All part of my day's work.

Schedule his diary, pacify his team, deal with irate customers, galvanise the sales force? Absolutely.

But could I point a wayward soul to his proper destination in the universe? Absolutely no flipping way. I didn't know where to begin.

I threw back the coffee, wishing it was something stronger, and was just about to go off for my shower when Jimmy appeared in the living room with the tiniest of towels covering his modesty and a huge grin upon his face.

'So, this is your sister then, is it? Aren't you going to introduce me?'

My mouth gaped opened, but words completely failed me. There was a near-naked man parading himself in my living room. A stunningly gorgeous one, at that. My stomach went into freefall as I looked from Jimmy across to Lexie, who was completely oblivious to my discomfort, before my gaze returned to Jimmy's resplendent form. I sighed inwardly, as my breath caught in my throat, desire trickling through my veins. This guy was known as a smooth operator; easy on the eye with an open charming manner, but in the flesh, up close and personal, his physical attributes were more captivating than I could ever have imagined.

It was all I could do to stop myself from screaming, 'Look, Lexie, have you clocked the pecs on that!'

Instead, I did another quick glance between Lexie and Jimmy and said, involuntarily, 'Lexie.'

'Yeah?' she quickly countered.

This was freaky. She must be able to see him, to catch the smile currently hovering on his lips, to hear his warm nut-brown voice ricocheting off the small walls of my flat. But she was totally oblivious to his overpowering physical presence.

'I'll just go and get ready then and we'll go, shall we?'

'Great. You don't mind if I switch on the telly while I'm waiting, do you?'

'No. You go ahead,' I said, backing out of the room as I watched Jimmy join my sister on the sofa. What she'd think about having an almost naked sex idol rubbing thighs with her, I didn't want to imagine.

'She looks nothing like you, does she?' he called, throwing a glance my way.

I shrugged and threw a glare back. What did he expect me to say?

'Won't be long!' Even I could hear the note of hysterical desperation in my voice.

To be honest, I couldn't wait to get out of the flat. Less than sixteen hours ago, Jimmy and I had been strangers. And now we were in the unenviable position of being stuck with each other for goodness knows how long. Like being fixed up on a blind date and knowing from the off that it was a non-starter, but still having to sit through the entire evening, making polite conversation.

I was in and out of the shower in a jiffy, threw on some jeans and my favourite pink jersey top and applied a quick covering of brown mascara to my lashes, a dab of bronzer to my cheeks and a lick of gloss to my lips.

'Okay, let's go,' I said, grabbing my handbag, but it seemed Lexie wasn't about to go anywhere.

'It's unbelievable, isn't it?' she said, zapping the TV off with the remote control and sighing exaggeratedly.

I was beginning to think, uncharitably, that Jimmy was revelling in all this attention. He looked across at me, a smug look upon his face, and shrugged his shoulders.

'What?' I said, not really needing to ask the question.

'Jimmy Mack. Dying like that. So suddenly. Who'd have thought it?'

'Hmm, I know, it's very sad,' I sighed, trying my best to muster up some sympathy, but to be frank, I was all sympathied out. Especially when the object of my sister's sympathy was sitting right next to her, wearing next to nothing, seemingly enjoying the fact that we were deep in discussion about him.

'You just wonder what really happened, don't you?'

'It doesn't bear thinking about,' I sighed. 'He probably just lost control at the wheel.'

'Hmm, it's a bit odd, though, isn't it? I mean, the road and weather conditions were perfect, so what caused him to come off the road like that? We probably don't know the half of it yet. Maybe he was into drink or drugs.'

'Oh, pleeaaase,' Jimmy said, so vehemently I was sure Lexie would hear.

'I don't think so,' I said. 'He didn't seem the type.'

Jimmy nodded approvingly.

'A lot of those celebrities are, you know. Perhaps he'd been at some drink and drugs-fuelled orgy and it sent him over the edge. Or maybe he was involved in some sordid sex scandal that was about to be exposed to the world and he topped himself.'

'Good grief, does your sister make a habit of slagging off poor unsuspecting celebrities? I've never touched drugs in my life. Okay, so maybe I like the odd glass of champagne. Who doesn't? But I certainly hadn't been drinking that day. Really!' He chewed on the inside of his lip, shaking his head at Lexie. 'Put her straight, would you, before I do her for defamation of character.'

I smiled, feeling thankful now that Lexie wasn't aware of Jimmy's overpowering near-naked presence after all.

'Jimmy was the real housewives' favourite. He couldn't be seen to be doing anything dodgy. Besides, he always seemed to me to be a true gentleman. Honest and caring. No, I can't imagine there were any skeletons in his cupboards.'

'Aw, that's such a nice thing to say.' Jimmy beamed under the weight of my compliment. 'Thanks, Alice.'

'Huh, and when did you become such a fan of JM anyway?' Lexie said, spoiling the moment. 'You always said he was a bit too smooth, a bit too squeaky clean. I don't like to speak ill of the dead, but honestly, I'd rather have Barney Roberts any time of the day.'

I paused, suddenly aware of Jimmy's laser-like stare bearing down on me. Lexie took my hesitation for complicit agreement.

'Come on, you have to admit Barney has something special going on.'

An awkward silence punctured the air as I searched for something to say.

'You have a thing for Barney Roberts?' Jimmy spat the words out as he ran his hands through his hair, looking indignant. 'Please tell me it isn't true. Really, Alice, if you knew him, you'd never think that way. The guy's a complete loser. What on earth would you see in him?'

I shrugged helplessly, giving up the search for something placatory to say.

Lexie, though, was in full-on swooning mode, as she examined her fingernails, deep in thought.

'I think he's really hot. Mmm, mmm. Young and sexy. A bit dangerous, too. I like that in a man. You know, that whole bad boy unpredictable thing.' She shivered exaggeratedly as if imagining doing unimaginable things with Barney.

Jimmy shook his head, tutting.

'What is this? The Barney Roberts Appreciation Society?'

'Come on,' I said, finding my voice at last, eager to separate the pair of them and lower the sizzling temperature within the flat, 'let's get going, before it gets too busy out there.'

I gave Jimmy a furtive little wave, then slammed the door shut on him and the flat for a few hours, grateful for a little respite from the huge problem that had bulldozed into my life. I took a deep breath. I would deal with it all later. Maybe by the time I got home, Jimmy would have received a communication from the powers upstairs.

4

Three hours, a lot of walking and four carrier bags – all belonging to Lexie – later, we settled at a pavement table outside a bustling café on the High Street. It was bright and the cold pinched my skin, but as the sun was making such a valiant attempt at breaking through the clouds, the least we felt we could do was make the most of the uncharacteristically good weather.

'You sure you're okay?' she asked through narrowed eyes. 'You seem, I don't know, a bit distracted, that's all.'

I shrugged and gave a non-committal smile.

The distractions were everywhere, but what could I possibly tell her?

I'd been determined to forget about Jimmy for a few hours at least, but that was proving impossible. Every newsstand, every paper, every television shop we passed in the street served as a reminder that I hadn't dreamt the whole mind-blowing episode up. Jimmy Mack was dead and, for reasons that I couldn't entirely fathom, he'd decided to make a detour on his way to the other side and camp out at my place for a while.

'You seem on edge, a bit strung out. You need to relax. Get out and enjoy yourself a bit more.'

I raised my eyebrows. She'd be strung out if her new lodger was a ghost. That sort of thing takes some getting used to.

Besides, I knew from experience exactly what Lexie had in mind when she talked about me enjoying myself more. I braced myself.

'I mean, how long has it been now, since Mike?'

She knew just as well as I did, but I humoured her.

'Oh, about three years, I suppose.' Three years,

six months and four days, to be precise. Not that I was counting.

'Exactly! Far too long. You need to get out there, move on, make a life for yourself.'

'I have a life, thank you very much,' I said, lowering my voice as I noticed the guy on the next table beginning to take an unnatural interest in our conversation.

'Yeah, but when was the last time you went out on a date? With a guy, I mean?'

'Hmm, well, that's what usually happens on a date, isn't it? You go out with a guy.' The pot of sugars on the table suddenly seemed very appealing. I picked up a bunch and turned them over in my fingers. 'And I've been out on lots of dates, it's just that I've never wanted to see any of them again.'

'Too fussy, that's your problem. You're waiting for your soulmate to fall out of the sky, but that's never going to happen, Alice. Life isn't a romantic novel, you know.'

I couldn't help smiling, especially after yesterday. Stranger things had definitely happened.

'You've got to give guys a chance,' she went on.

'Get to know them. They're not all like Mike, you know. There are some decent ones out there.'

What she meant was that they weren't all two-timing, lying little toerags like my ex. That was maybe the case, although I wasn't still entirely convinced on that point, but I really didn't have the time or the inclination to get involved with anyone at the moment. Besides, entertaining the idea of a boyfriend was out of the question now. I had an unexpected house guest to look after.

'Maybe,' I said, unable to hide my scepticism, 'but you can't force these things. If it's meant to happen, it will.'

Leaving it to fate, I'd decided, was a much better option than road-testing a whole string of Mr Maybes, Mr Highly Unlikelys and Mr Downright Unsuitables.

Just then, a jet of cold air whooshed around my neck and whipped up my trouser legs.

'Not interrupting anything, am I?'

'Oh, my God!' I jumped in my seat, knocking the remains of my cappuccino over the small table. Wildly, I looked around, half expecting the entire

High Street to be looking my way, but there was only Lexie, who was observing me oddly.

'See, just look at you. You're so uptight and edgy.' She made a half-hearted attempt at mopping up the coffee with some paper napkins. 'What on earth's the matter with you?'

At least Jimmy had the grace to look sheepish.

'You don't mind if I join you?' he said, slipping into the chair beside me, not looking remotely interested in my answer.

'Nothing,' I said to Lexie, my gaze scouring the neighbouring tables to see if anybody had noticed the arrival of Jimmy Mack, but there wasn't a flicker of interest from any quarter. I was slowly coming to terms with the weird fact that Jimmy was visible only to me.

'I thought I felt something on my arm, something crawly,' I said, trying to keep the hysteria from my voice. 'Must have imagined it!'

When Jimmy shuffled his chair closer to mine, I noticed Lexie's incredulous gaze settle on his ghostly form. For a split second, I thought we were busted, but quickly realised it wasn't Jimmy she was seeing, but the chair, seemingly moving of its own accord. Swiftly, I hooked my foot around the leg of the chair and yanked it frantically from side to side.

'There! I told you. It was a spider. Got it,' I said, with a triumphant sigh, screwing my foot into the ground.

Lexie's brow furrowed and her mouth twisted in disbelief at my suspect behaviour. When she stood up, shaking her head, I breathed a huge sigh of relief.

'I'm just popping to the loo, and then we'll go, shall we? Before we get thrown out of this place.'

I nodded with an apologetic smile and picked up my handbag, turning my attention to Jimmy as soon as Lexie had left.

'You gave me the fright of my life popping up like that.' I was doing my best impression of a ventriloquist for the benefit of the man on the next table. 'You could have given me some warning,' I hissed. 'What did you expect me to say?'

'Sorry,' he laughed, 'but you have to remember I'm finding my way around this whole thing too. I didn't realise I could transport myself from one place to the other just by the power of thought. Look at this,' he said, sounding unnecessarily excited.

'Abracadabra!' He waved his arms in the air with a dramatic flourish before disappearing into thin air and reappearing over the other side of the patio area, squeezed between two fat ladies enjoying a morning croissant. He gave me a little wave, before repeating his magic chant.

'That's pretty cool, isn't it?' He popped up again beside me. 'Obviously I don't need to say "Abracadabra", but I think it brings a certain "je ne sais quoi" to the overall effect, don't you?'

'Very clever,' I said, feeling secretly impressed and annoyed all at the same time. I still wasn't entirely convinced I wasn't hallucinating. 'How did you know where to find me, though?'

'I didn't. I was just thinking about you. It was pretty lonely cooped up in that flat of yours and I was wondering when you'd be back and then suddenly, whoosh, and I was here.' He laughed, obviously reliving the moment.

'Blimey, that is pretty freaky, but I suppose it has its benefits. Saves all that hassle of getting on buses and tubes,' I joked.

'Yeah,' he said, his expression falling. 'The only

downside is you have to be dead to qualify for the perk. Might be a bit of a drastic move just to avoid the rush-hour traffic. Mind if I help myself to one of these biscuits?'

I watched as he greedily devoured not one, but the three remaining biscuits on the plate, the man on the next table spluttering over his coffee as the biscuits evaporated into thin air.

'Mmm, lovely,' I said, smiling sweetly, making exaggerated chewing motions in an attempt to cover up Jimmy's greediness, before twisting my chair and turning my back on the man sitting beside us.

'That's seriously weird,' I said to Jimmy, watching him as if I'd never seen someone eating before.

'Huh?' he asked, through a mouthful of crumbs.

'How you have to do the whole eating and drinking and sleeping thing. I thought... well, you don't expect...' My voice trailed away at the ridiculousness of this conversation.

'What? All those other ghosts you've met haven't needed to do that, then? Well, I must be special.' With his grey eyes wide with mischief and a smile hovering on his lips, there was no way I could disagree on that fact.

'Well, it doesn't happen in the films,' I said, determined not to be distracted by his obscenely good looks.

'This isn't a film, Alice. This is your terrifying new reality.' He chuckled and leant over, blowing a kiss on my nose. 'I wonder if it's because I haven't passed over yet. I guess all this wafting around in no man's land requires a certain amount of energy. Once I get over to the other side, I'm sure this whole maintenance thing will be redundant. It's just a case of me getting there.' He flashed me another smile, the one that said 'we're in this together, kiddo'.

'Well, I'm not sure why you've decided I'm the person to help you get to the other side,' I muttered, a tad petulantly. 'I haven't got a clue what you should do and it's not as if I have any spiritual leanings, either. The last time I was in a church was at my cousin's wedding and I didn't really pay any attention to the business side of things.'

He leant across the table and laid his hand on mine. It was the most peculiar experience. It felt so natural and yet otherworldly at the same time, sending shivers rippling down my spine.

'I didn't decide on you, Alice. That's the thing. You've been specially selected for the job. A bit like those *Reader's Digest* promotions your nan used to get through the post. Obviously, someone, somewhere thinks you have something to teach me.'

I gulped at the enormity of the situation as the guy from the next-door table gave me a very dubious look. Well, as far as he was concerned, I'd been talking to myself for the last five minutes, as well as demolishing everything in sight on the food front; he probably had me down as a complete basket case.

What on earth was it that I, Alice Fletcher, could teach Jimmy Mack?

'Shall we go, then?' Lexie was back, her wide smile bringing a welcome touch of reality into my world.

'Great.' I stood up, picking up my bag before looking back at Jimmy.

'Don't worry about me,' he said, flashing me that smile again. 'I'll make my own way back. I'll probably make it before you. Abracadabra and all that!'

He winked and I watched him evaporate into thin air. That really was some party trick. I couldn't help giggling, and the guy at the table next door quickly looked away, finding his weighty paperback suddenly very interesting, just when I caught him looking at me again.

Mad greedy women were to be avoided at all costs, obviously.

5

Not only did Jimmy make it back home before me, but he was also thoughtful enough to have cleared the mess away, washed up the dirty crockery and made his bed. A piping hot cup of tea was waiting for me on the kitchen table.

'I could get used to this kind of thing,' I said, smiling, dropping my handbag on the floor. For the briefest moment, the thought of sharing my life with someone who would be waiting for me at the end of a hard day with a warm welcome and a glass of something special in hand seemed very appealing. Someone like Jimmy, I thought in a moment of wild fantasy, as our eyes met across the kitchen. I fought the urge to run into his arms and attack him with a barrage of kisses.

'That's good, because you might have to,' he said, without any trace of humour, clearly not on the same wavelength as me. 'For a little while, at least. It must seem extremely rude, me gatecrashing your life uninvited, but hopefully it won't be for long. Once we find out where I'm supposed to be going, then I'll be out of your hair for good. And you can forget that you ever met me.'

I snorted – that was highly unlikely. How would I ever forget Jimmy? I hadn't met a ghost before, especially one with such a high profile as Jimmy Mack, so it's not exactly something that would easily slip my mind.

'Don't worry,' I said. 'We'll work something out.' I sank down on the sofa, realising my plans for having a chilled-out vegging weekend would have to be put on hold. In fact, all plans were on hold for the foreseeable future. I wasn't entirely disappointed by the fact.

'I promise, as soon as I can, I'll be out of your way. I could go now if you really wanted me to. Find somewhere to hang out. Do what ghosts do, I suppose.' He shrugged, smiling. 'Do a bit of haunting in my spare time. Get my own back on all those people who pissed me off in life.'

'Don't be silly,' I said, casting him a grave glance. 'You'd get lonely with no one to talk to. I've heard about unhappy ghosts and the havoc they can cause. No, you're much better here with me. Where I can keep an eye on you. Together, we can work out what we're supposed to do with you.'

Although Lord knew what that might be. I scratched my head, frustrated at my lack of re-sourcefulness. I was way out of my depth, crazily so.

I didn't want to think about it too closely, but this had to be a commonplace occurrence. People died every day. I was certain they didn't all go through this stage, wafting around in the ether, at-taching themselves to some poor unsuspecting human until they had the go-ahead to move on to wherever they were supposed to be going. No, something had clearly gone very wrong in Jimmy's transition and if we didn't do something about it soon, he could be trapped here like this forever.

'We need to go back to the crash scene,' I said, with a sudden sense of urgency.

'What are you talking about?'

'The accident! That was where your spirit should have been collected from. I don't know why it wasn't, probably an oversight or something, but maybe if we get you back there, then they'll come for you and you can... um... get taken across... to... well, um, you know.'

'Hmm, you make it sound like the dustbin collections. If they don't pick up one week, they'll catch you second time around. I'm not sure it quite works like that.'

'Do you have any better ideas?' I snapped.

Jimmy sighed, dropping his head backwards and gazing up at the ceiling.

'No, not at the moment, I don't. I'm just trying to lighten the atmosphere, that's all.'

'Well, in that case, if you don't mind, can we have a go at doing things my way please?'

* * *

'Do I have to come?'

I'd pulled the car over to the side of the road where I'd stopped only yesterday, not knowing at that point that my life was about to take such a weirdly unexpected turn. In the half-light, the field gave no clue to the horrors it had witnessed, but the stillness that had been so apparent in daylight only seemed magnified in the eerie twilight.

'Don't be ridiculous. Of course you have to come. What would be the point in me going on my own? It's you that we're trying to get dispatched, after all.'

Jimmy winced, looking at me through narrowed eyes, and I immediately regretted my choice of words. To be honest, I wanted nothing more than to turn around and take him home to the safety of my flat, but I knew that wouldn't have helped either of us.

'I'm just not sure this is a good idea, that's all. For goodness' sake, Alice, this is where it all happened. I really don't think I need to be revisiting the scene of my death. It's too soon, it's not right.'

I turned my head to look at him and he grasped my hand, as though it were the most natural thing in the world, our fingers instantly interlocking.

'I know this is difficult, Jimmy, but you being stuck in this state of limbo isn't right either. I'm worried for you. This has been devastating for everyone concerned, but we can't change what's happened. What we can do is try our hardest to make sure you end up where you should be and I'm pretty certain that isn't meant to be in my little flat. You should be out there,' I pointed into the distance through the windscreen, 'with your own... your own type.'

I cringed. He cringed. There was no easy way to say these things.

'You make it sound so very appealing.' He laughed, tipping his head back on the car seat. His strongly defined jawline, the tilt of his chin, the tiny dimple at the corner of his mouth were highlighted in profile, making my heart twist with longing.

'Come on,' he said, leaning over and tracing a finger down the length of my cheek. 'Let's get this over with, then.'

Outside, the sky had darkened further, and I dug my hands into my jacket pockets wondering why I'd ever thought this was a good idea. An icy chill ran down the length of my body as my eyes searched out the spot where the wreckage had strewn the countryside.

'At least the car has gone now.'

'Yeah, I really loved that car,' he said wistfully. 'I'd only had it three months. Just had it valeted too. Still, I don't suppose I'd have much use for it now.'

'Don't think about it,' I said feeling guilty that I was putting him through such an ordeal. 'It was over there.' I led him by the hand across the uneven ground, trying to work out the least hazardous path in the darkness. 'This phone is useless!' I stopped to check that it was actually working, the beam from the torch so feeble we could barely see a thing. I turned it off in frustration. 'I don't suppose you have a torch with you, do you?'

'Oh, yes, I have one right here in my jacket pocket,' he said tightly. 'No, Alice, I do not have a torch with me.'

'All right, it was only an idea. Look we're here now anyway. You can see the flattened grass. See.' I bent down, sweeping my palm across the ground.

'Great. Brings back such happy memories.' Jimmy wrapped his arms around his chest, looking totally disinterested. 'So, what do you suggest we do now, then?'

'I think we need to take a moment of silent reflection. Give thanks for your life and then ask our spirit friends to guide you on your way.'

Jimmy sniggered, looking around him.

'Well, all those other dudes obviously forgot to turn up. Perhaps they took the date down wrong in their diaries.'

'It isn't funny, Jimmy! You have to want to do this. It has to be worth a try.'

I grabbed his hands in mine, closed my eyes and took a couple of deep breaths.

'Friends, spirits—'

'Countrymen!' interrupted Jimmy.

'Stop it!' I hissed. 'We come in peace and friendship. We give thanks for the life of Jimmy Mack, who has now sadly departed from the physical realm. Please help us guide Jimmy to his rightful place in the universe.' I offered his hands up to the night sky. I knew the wording wasn't spot on, but I just hoped someone somewhere would get the gist.

We stood there in the increasing cold a moment or two longer, before he dropped his hands to his sides.

'Nice try, Alice, and I do appreciate all the trouble you've gone to, but really, this isn't going to work. Can we go home, please? I'm freezing cold, hungry and tired. I can think of much better ways we could be spending our time.'

His gaze skittered over my face, and I wasn't sure about any of those other spirits, but mine plummeted to the floor. Tears gathered in my eyes. What had I been thinking? Jimmy was right, this was never going to work, and yet he'd been lovely enough to humour me and see this whole ridiculous escapade through to the end.

'Yes, I suppose you're right,' I sighed, defeated. 'We'll go. This is obviously not the way to do it, but there'll be another way. I promise you.'

Just as we turned to go, I spotted the lights in the distance. Vast bright white lights approaching at a steady pace, searching us out, the accompanying growling rumble growing louder and louder. I shielded my eyes with my arm from the dazzling glare, the vibrations from the craft reaching my shivering body.

'See, what did I tell you! Look! They've come for you, Jimmy. They've come for you.' Our eyes locked together and, in that moment, I realised that however important it was for Jimmy to find his spiritual home, I didn't want him to go. Not yet. I'd only just met him, but in some ways, it felt as if I'd known him a lifetime. And that wasn't nearly enough time. There was so much I still needed to know. The fact that I wanted him to stay, wanted more of him, filled me with fear. Why did I feel this way about a ghostly stranger? It didn't make any sense.

Emotion prickled through my entire body as I grabbed hold of his hand. The enormity of the situation was clearly too much for him as well as his whole body rocked with something approaching hysteria as he gasped to find the words.

'It's okay, it's okay,' I soothed, stroking his arm.

The craft shuddered to a halt in front of us and a door flew open, a man in overalls leaping down onto the ground.

'What the bloody hell do you think you're doing? In my bloody field! There's nothing to see here. The party's over. Now clear off!' he yelled.

I looked across at Jimmy who, doubled up with mirth, was no use whatsoever. Making abject apologies to the tractor driver, the ghost and I sprinted back to the car.

* * *

Okay, so Plan A may have been a major fail, but I was certain that there were dozens of other options we could try and in the meantime it wouldn't be too much of a hardship sharing the flat with Jimmy.

He was well-mannered, domesticated and easy on the eye. I'd had worse house guests.

As long as Jimmy obeyed a few simple house rules, then I couldn't foresee any problems. And the first and most important rule on the list, not to turn up unexpectedly when I was out doing other stuff, I reminded him of on Monday morning as I was getting ready to go to work.

'Now remember, you can't just turn up at work, showing off your fancy magic tricks. I have a very important job to do, and I really don't need the distraction of you popping up in the middle of an important board meeting.'

'Wow,' he said, letting out a slow whistle as his gaze travelled the length of my body, taking in my grey slub silk pencil skirt and matching jacket. His eyes lingered on my ankles and black patent court shoes. 'You look pretty hot in all that office gear.

Kind of severe and buttoned up, but I like that.' He raised his eyebrows approvingly and I turned away, trying to hide the fetching pink patches of embarrassment that were now adorning my cheeks. Jimmy Mack had a reputation as a flirt, only I would never have believed he'd be practising his skills on me. 'Very nice indeed,' he added.

'No turning up at the wrong times, Jimmy. Are you listening to me?' I asked, picking up my keys from the hall table, trying to ignore the warm fuzzy feeling his attention provoked.

'Yeah, yeah, don't worry, I'll be as good as gold. I promise. I've plenty to be getting on with here, anyway.' I couldn't imagine what. Maybe he had some ideas of his own about moving on to his rightful place.

'Good,' I said, on my way out. 'I'll see you later, then.'

'Yeah, you have a good day at the office, sweetie!'

6

'Morning, Alice, good weekend?'

Simon, my boss, had his sleeves rolled up and two empty coffee cups on his desk, suggesting he'd already been at work for at least a couple of hours.

'Yes, great,' I said opting for the sanitised version, not the 'you'll never believe it, but, a ghost moved into my flat, you might know him, he just happens to be a celebrity, and we spent the rest of the weekend trying to get rid of him again' version. Although that might have been fun just to see the look on Simon's face.

'Good, good,' he said, distracted. 'I'm in meetings for the best part of the day, but I've sent you a few tasks to your inbox if you could look at those for me. Oh, and you'll need to schedule in a meeting with Roger Carter. Damon Mitchell has been in this morning to hand in his resignation, so I'll need to chat through the likely ramifications with Roger.'

'Really?' I said, completely taken aback by the pang of disappointment the news elicited within me.

'Yep. Didn't see that one coming. He's our best salesman by a long chalk. I'm sorry to lose him, but he wasn't going to be bought off. He's leaving to start his own business, apparently. Landscape gardening. At least he's not going to one of our competitors. That would have really pissed me off.'

'I'll be sad to see him go,' I admitted, trying to wrestle the idea of the super-smooth salesman I knew giving up the suave designer suits for wellies and the outdoor life.

'Me too,' Simon said, as he turned to leave my office. 'I'll catch up with you at lunchtime if there's anything important.'

I realised with a thud that I'd miss seeing Damon about the place. His smiling face popping around my office door always lifted my spirits; he was funny, delightfully indiscreet, and yet always seemed genuinely pleased to see me, his cheeky banter never seeming intrusive, only affectionate.

I hated change, any kind of change, and all of a sudden, everything in my life seemed to be shifting like the earth's plates, creating imperceptible but far-reaching consequences.

Decisively, I clicked on my inbox, moving emails into folders, checking off tasks, my mind operating on autopilot. I glanced at my watch. It was two hours since I'd left Jimmy on his own and my attempts at not thinking about him were clearly failing. I'd been scared I might conjure him up in my office and I certainly didn't need that kind of distraction, but with him constantly in my thoughts and the news of Damon's departure rattling around in my head, it was almost impossible to concentrate on anything else.

What was Jimmy up to, I wondered, a lonely spirit navigating a hostile world?

I'd once signed up to an online dating agency, so I had a small idea how that felt, but however much I tried to imagine myself in Jimmy's shoes, I couldn't. It was too awful even to contemplate. How must he be feeling with no one to talk to or confide in? I only hoped he wouldn't do anything silly in my absence, but even that thought was ridiculous. He was hardly about to throw himself off a bridge or under a train. The worst had already happened.

Even so, when I walked back through my front door that night, it was a huge relief to find that Jimmy was still there, and to be greeted by the most delightful cooking smells wafting from the kitchen was an added bonus.

'Hey, you're home! Good day?' Jimmy welcomed me from the kitchen doorway wearing black chinos, a tightly fitted white T-shirt, my pinny and a big grin. Simple but dazzlingly effective. He looked as if he could have just wandered off a film set, the sight sending a ripple of excitement fizzing along the length of my body. His gaze appraised me, and his mouth parted as if he were about to say something before he obviously thought better of it.

'New clothes?' I asked, dropping my gaze. Either that, or he must have had an account with a laundry somewhere.

'My old clothes,' he said, matter-of-factly.

'Really? What, did you go back for them or something?'

'No. I got them sent over,' he said casually, as if this was indeed the Heavenly Hilton. My brow furrowed in confusion as I looked for clarification. 'I couldn't stay in those old things, the whiff of diesel and cowpats wasn't a great combination, so I, um, willed them over. A new start and everything.'

'You willed them over?' I gave a nervous giggle. 'How did you do that, exactly?'

Jimmy laughed too, turning his attention back to the frying pan.

'Well, I'm not sure about the technicalities, but in the same way that I can transport myself from one place to another, I can do the same thing with projecting an alternative form of myself. This is my casual day look,' he said with a wry grin, striking a pose. 'Do you like it?'

'I do,' I said, sounding like a star-struck fan, but still struggling to get my head round what he was telling me. 'So you don't actually change your clothes at all. I'm just seeing, what, a different version of you?'

'You got it!' he said, as though that was a per-

fectly reasonable explanation. If it wasn't for the seriously impressive magic tricks, then it would have
been easy to forget that Jimmy was a ghost. He was
such a vibrant, larger-than-life force, occupying my
flat and now my head and part of my heart too.

'Something smells good.' My nostrils picked out
the aromas of garlic, tomatoes and onions. 'You
didn't need to go to all this trouble.'

'It's the least I could do after everything you've
done for me. It's just pasta with a tomato sauce. I
hope that's okay?'

'Sounds perfect,' I said, accepting the glass of
chilled white sparkling wine he was offering. Our
glasses clinked, our eyes meeting as we took a sip
together, the bubbles on my tongue matching my
own fizzing excitement. 'What about you? How was
your day?'

'Yeah, not bad. Although I missed you, Alice.'
His expression was deadly serious, but his eyes
twinkled with mischievousness. 'I did a bit of cleaning.' He gestured around him at the gleaming surfaces. 'I hope you don't mind?'

'No.' I shook my head in amazement. 'Anytime
you get the urge, you go straight ahead.' I laughed,

feeling a pang of guilt that he'd had to resort to getting the duster out. I couldn't see him sticking out this new role for long. Going from being a feted celebrity to my domestic lackey didn't seem like the best career move in the world.

In my own flat, I felt redundant, wondering what I should do next. I looked around at the uncharacteristically spotless living room and settled myself on the sofa, trying not to mess up the careful display of cushions. For some reason, I felt vaguely nervous, as though I was waiting for a job interview.

'Can I help at all?' It was a half-hearted offer, but one that went a small way to making me feel better. I slipped off my shoes and kicked them under the coffee table, trying for relaxed.

'No,' he said, turning and giving me an indulgent smile. 'It's all under control. Just sit back and enjoy.'

'So where did you learn to cook, then?' I asked a bit later, when we were sitting at the table, tucking eagerly into the tagliatelle. I hadn't realised how hungry I was.

'At uni. I had a few months living off Pot Noodles, and then decided, for the sake of my health, I needed to learn a few basic dishes that included some green stuff. Thinking about it, I needn't have worried. Could have stuffed myself silly with burgers, fries and beers.' He gave a wry shrug. 'Funny how you spend a lot of time sparing yourself for the future when in a lot of cases there won't be a future. Let that be a lesson to you, Alice.' He pointed a friendly finger my way. 'Get out there and live your life to the full, young lady. And eat as many burgers and fries as you want to.'

I laughed, my insides squirming uncomfortably at the further reminder of Jimmy's perilous condition.

'Hmm, trouble is, knowing my luck, I'd do exactly that, put on sixteen stone, become an alcoholic bag lady and live to 105. Very old, very fat, drunk and lonely with no one to care for me.'

'Now that is hard to imagine. But you know what I'm saying, don't you?' There was a sincerity in his voice which was hard to ignore. 'Make the most of what you've got, your time here, because it could all be over in an instant.' He clicked his fingers in the air. 'Work out what's important to you and go for it.'

I twirled my pasta around my fork absentmindedly. That was easy for him to say, but then I guessed he had the benefit of hindsight; he was looking at it from the other side. Literally. Like a lot of people, I had a vague idea of the things I wanted from life, but most of those I had pencilled in for some time in the future. But what if my future were to be cut short, like Jimmy's? A feeling of unease, tempered with impatience, niggled along my veins.

'Do it, Alice, before it's too late,' he said, as if reading my mind. 'It's all too easy to put things off, but my advice to you is to go out there and grab life with both hands. And it's not things like your career and money that are important, you know that. It's your friends and family.' He paused. 'Your relationships.'

I laughed, looking up into his eyes.

'Oh dear, you're beginning to sound like my mother. And my sister.'

'Really? I'm in good company, then. What is it they say exactly?'

'That I should get out more. Start dating again. I

think they'd like to see me settled with someone. It's been a while since Mike.'

'Mike?'

'Yeah, he was my last serious relationship. We were together for about five years and everyone thought we would have the happy ending, but it wasn't to be. We sort of fizzled out.' I laughed without a smidgen of self-consciousness. It was such a long time ago now, it was almost like talking about another person. 'That's not strictly true. Not so much a fizzle as an explosion when I found out he was cheating on me with a couple of other girls. I haven't really got back into the dating scene since.'

'His loss, definitely,' said Jimmy, looking at me intently from beneath long dark lashes. 'There'll be some good guy out there for you, Alice. Someone you can be happy with. You're such a great girl, you deserve to be happy, but you need to get out there and find him. Take it from me, you don't have as much time here as you might think.'

'I suppose you're right,' I said with a pang of regret. It felt so easy to be talking with Jimmy, safe and reassuring, as if I could tell him anything and he would never judge me in any way. Perhaps that was because I knew he wasn't of this world. That we had something special and sacred that would only ever exist between the two of us. How many conversations did we have left, I wondered, before Jimmy would leave our strange twilight world forever?

'That's what they say, isn't it? You don't get to your deathbed wishing you spent more time in the office. Was there someone special in your life?' I probed again. 'Someone you wished you'd spent more time with.'

'No, sadly not.' Now it was Jimmy's turn to look pensive. 'I wish there had been. It was all up here.' He tapped the side of his head. 'My master plan for the future. I had it all mapped out: a mad, passionate love affair with the woman who was to be my wife, a couple of kids, an apartment in town, the big house in the country, a golden retriever, guinea pig, the full works. Only I got stuck at first base. I didn't get to meet the woman of my dreams.'

'That's so sad.' Tears pricked at the back of my eyes, but I blinked them away. It was such a terrible waste. Jimmy would have made a wonderful husband and a fantastic father too, I didn't doubt. And now it was too late for him.

'Actually,' he said, putting his fork and spoon down, 'there was something I wanted to ask you.'

'Of course. Just ask away,' I said lightly, trying to ignore the growing sense of trepidation in my tummy.

'I wondered if you'd come with me, when all the arrangements have been made?'

'Come with you?'

'Yes, to the funeral. I need to be there, obviously, but I don't think I can face it alone. It would mean a lot to me if you came along.'

I hoped Jimmy hadn't noticed my sharp intake of breath. It hadn't occurred to me that he'd go to the funeral, well, not in a wafting-around capacity, at least, and surely I'd be conspicuous, not knowing anyone else in the congregation.

'It's okay,' he said, doing that weird thing of seemingly reading my mind again, 'you can say you were a good friend of mine. There are a lot of friends my family hadn't got to meet. Please, Alice?'

'Of course I'll come,' I said, feeling honoured to be asked. 'I can book the day off work. It should be fine.'

'Thanks.' Jimmy smiled, looking relieved, and

reached across the table, his hand finding mine. My
fingers sizzled, my whole body warming from the
intimacy of his touch.

Something stirred deep inside me as my eyes
locked with Jimmy's. I was the only one he had now,
the only person in this world who could help him,
and I wanted to ensure I did everything in my
power to do exactly that.

* * *

I hated lying but it was a case of having to when I
popped into my boss's office the following week. I
rarely took time off, so Simon was more than happy
to accommodate my request, especially when I told
him it was to attend a funeral.

'I'm sorry to hear that, Alice. It wasn't anybody
close, was it?' He'd looked up from his papers, genuine concern etched across his brow.

'Um, a cousin, twice removed, on my mother's
side. I hadn't seen her in ages. But we were close. As
children. Well, I was a child and she was a bit older
and then we grew up, of course.' *Shut up now*, I told
myself, but my mouth had gone into hyperactive

mode. 'And then she died. Just like that. Very unexpectedly. So sad.'

'That is very sad,' said Simon. 'Well, if you need to take any extra time off, then you only have to ask.'

'Oooh, thank you,' I said, a little over-enthusiastically, as if he'd agreed to me going off on some jolly. 'I just need Friday off. That's all. I'll be back on Monday.' I took a deep breath in an attempt to lose the hysterical edge to my voice. I was absolutely hopeless at this lying lark. I always felt everyone could see straight through me as soon as any untruth left my lips, and I have to admit Simon was observing me sceptically over the top of his glasses.

'If you're sure.'

Hopefully, he'd put my manic, out-of-character behaviour down to the distress of losing my much-loved, if distant, aunt. Or was it my cousin? I needed to be sure of that fact.

He got up from behind his desk and came over and squeezed my shoulder. I nodded in thanks and turned and walked out of his office. I was sure I could hear his huge sigh of relief.

Back at my desk, I settled myself in my chair and checked my inbox.

From: Damon Mitchell
To: Alice Fletcher
Subject: My Leaving Do
Hey, Alice, we're having a few drinks next Saturday evening at The Grapes. About 6.00 pm till chucking out time. I hope you'll join us. Please? I don't want any of your lame excuses either.

I fired off a quick reply.

To: Damon Mitchell
From: Alice Fletcher
Subject: Re: My Leaving Do
Damon, I don't know what you mean about my lame excuses! I wouldn't miss your leaving do for the world. Looking forward to it. A.

My gaze travelled down the list of unread emails.

From: Susannah Orbin, Head of Corporate Entertaining

To: Alice Fletcher, PA to Simon Ibbotson

Subject: Charity Ball

Just to let you know, following Jimmy Mack's untimely death, that we have been able to secure the
services of Barney Roberts to act as a replacement
auctioneer at the forthcoming Charity Ball. With the
short timescale involved, I hope you'll agree that we
have been extremely fortuitous in being able to book
an equally high-profile celebrity to take Jimmy's
place. I'm sure the success of the ball won't be
compromised in any way. Please let me know if
there are any problems with this minor change in the
arrangements. Kind Regards. Susannah.

Unbidden, tears filled my eyes. The words
blurred before me as I read them again, trying to
make sense of their meaning. Jimmy had been
booked for the Charity Ball? It came like a thund-
erbolt from the sky. To think that for the matter of a
few weeks our paths would have crossed in real life.
It tore at my heart to think that I could have met
Jimmy in different circumstances entirely.

Through my tears, I read the email again, the

tone making my skin prickle with distaste. How could she dismiss him like that in a couple of sentences? A minor change to the arrangements! It was so much more than that. To all the people who'd loved Jimmy, his fanbase, his friends and family, his passing would leave a huge hole in their lives that could never be filled. The fact that some stupid bloody woman could think he was so easily replaceable enraged me. Why didn't she care? I cared. Sitting there at my desk, I realised I cared so much more than I would ever have thought possible.

'Alice, are you sure you're okay? Why don't you go home early?' I hadn't heard Simon come up behind me. Hastily wiping my face with the tissue I recovered from up my sleeve, I nodded.

'I'm fine, Simon, really. Just an allergy, I think,' I said unconvincingly, as I attempted to mop up my sodden face. Simon nodded in sympathy, looking as though he'd rather be anywhere else than standing over his frankly hopeless PA today. I made a muffled attempt at communication.

'I was just coming back to see you actually. *SNIFF*. I've got some appointments I'd like to confirm for the diary. *SNIFF*. And, just so as you know,

Corporate Entertaining have been in touch to say they've arranged for Barney Roberts to appear as Auctioneer at the Ball. *SNIFF SNIFF.*'

'Ah yes, of course. We had Jimmy Mack down for that, didn't we? Terrible thing to have happened.' He shook his head. 'At his age, too.'

At the mention of his name, I couldn't hold it together a moment longer. I broke down into gulping sobs, my whole body shuddering as I looked up at Simon's stricken face, the full implication of what had happened to Jimmy finally hitting me hard in the chest.

'Really, Alice, I insist. You need to go home. Take a couple of days, as long as you need. There's nothing here so urgent that it can't wait until you get back.'

When I walked out of the door, still sniffing, I don't know who was more relieved, me or my clearly shaken boss, Simon.

7

Mettlesham was the quintessential English village; pretty cottages with picket gates and thatched roofs dotted around the village green, a pub, the White Hart, that had held centre stage for a couple of hundred years at least, and a Saxon church nestling amongst oak and yew trees. Normally, according to Jimmy, this sleepy little hamlet played host to the very occasional visitor, curious only about the history of the church, or daytrippers sampling the delights of the local inn, but today it was swarming with family and friends of James McArthur, who had come to pay their respects. It was supposed to be a small family affair, but I conservatively estimated the crowds to be in the hundreds.

Jimmy had told me about growing up in Mettlesham, about the little village school he'd attended before moving on to the grammar school, a bus ride away in the next big town. It was funny to think I was standing in a place where he'd spent so many happy times, among people I didn't know, but who had played such an important part in his life.

Jimmy was giving me a running commentary on who was who as the procession of mourners filed into the church.

'That's Mrs Butterworth,' he said, pointing out a large lady in a floaty black skirt and blouse. 'She was my first teacher at school. Very strict, but a complete sweetheart beneath that slightly scary exterior. Look,' he whispered in my ear, causing the hairs to rise on my neck. 'There's Uncle Harry! I used to spend my summers when I was a boy helping out on his farm. Oh, and there's Grandma Rose. Aw, she looks so frail,' he added wistfully. 'I hope she's okay.'

A tall willowy lady hung onto Harry's arm for

support, resembling a sunflower lowering its head in deference to the change in season.

'Those two over there are Paul and Sylvia, our next-door neighbours. I was best friends with their kids Natalie and Ryan. I spent more time in their house than I ever did in mine. They held the best Christmas parties. Ah, I'm going to miss those guys so much.'

'They'll miss you too, Jimmy,' I said, barely able to keep a lid on the emotion bubbling beneath my skin. I felt privileged to be here at Jimmy's side, but an all-pervading sense of sadness swept through me like a tidal wave.

'Mum, Dad!' he said, his voice breaking with emotion. There was no mistaking his parents, Rosemary and Michael, carrying themselves with a quiet dignity as they greeted the other mourners.

I grabbed hold of Jimmy's hand and squeezed it tight, biting on my lip to stop the tears from falling. The sight of his parents, their bodies clearly racked with grief, was almost too much to witness.

'You look just like your dad.' The older, more distinguished, version of Jimmy looked across at me and, although we'd never met before, our eyes locked for a moment in what I hoped was a shared understanding and purpose.

'Everyone says so.' Jimmy gave a rueful smile. 'I think I'm more like my mum in temperament though. We are very close – we were very close,' he corrected himself. 'And they are the perfect couple, they have the happiest of marriages. It was what I aspired to and I think probably the reason I never got round to settling down. I was hanging out for The One.' Jimmy lifted my hand to his lips, brushing the lightest of kisses against my fingertips, and I felt my whole body sway against him. 'Thanks, Alice. For being here. It means so much.'

'Come on,' I said, smiling, wondering how I'd ever get through this day. 'I think we probably need to go in now.'

'It's weird to think all these people have turned out for me.' He paused, looking all around him. 'Really weird. Half of them I don't even recognise.'

'Well, they obviously know you, Jimmy. They've come to say goodbye. It just goes to show how much you meant to so many people.'

'Yeah,' he sighed, wistfully. 'That's pretty cool,

isn't it? Will you be okay if I wander off for a while? There's something I need to do.'

'Yes, of course,' I whispered beneath my breath, not wanting to draw any unnecessary attention. 'You go.' I felt his fingers slip through mine and my heart knotted as I watched him leave.

Surely the others would see him, I thought, my heart thumping in my chest. He was there, as apparent to me as the carved angels on the oak beams stretching across the eaves and the tall stained-glass windows throwing sunlight down the nave, his distinctive rangy frame casting a seemingly huge shadow. I wanted to run after him, to call his name, to see him turn to look at me with that huge wide smile upon his face, but all I could do was look on helplessly.

The sunlit patterns spreading down the aisle brought a flash of clarity. What if this was it? It hadn't occurred to me before, but it made perfect sense now. That his spirit should be reunited with his body in the beautiful surroundings of the majestic church, with all the people he knew and loved around him. It seemed such a fitting tribute. The perfect solution to our problem, too. And yet if this was it, I knew I'd be losing Jimmy forever. That I'd never get to see or speak to him again. My heart twisted in pain, my arms aching to reach out for him.

He slipped into the space between his mother and father and his head fell onto his mum's shoulder. I saw her turn towards him as if she knew he was there, the tension and grief held rigid in her shoulders escaping from her body in that moment. They stayed like that, perfectly still, completely at one with each other. With tears falling down my cheeks, I couldn't drag my eyes away from them.

It was a beautiful service, simple and touching. There were readings from his best friend and the producer of his TV show, Justin Dawkins, and Paul, the next-door neighbour, whose fragile emotions had the congregation hanging onto his every word. Ryan managed to lighten the mood with his tales of the antics of two schoolboys and friends, and the mischief and mayhem they managed to cause in the long summer holidays.

'Jimmy was, as every single person here will know, a very special person. Not just through his on-screen persona, but as a son, grandson, colleague and, of course, a friend.' He paused, biting on his lip, his eyes moistened with emotion. 'He was my best friend. Even as a young boy, that special quality that would be so evident in his later life to so many people could be seen shining through. He was, to my great displeasure at the time, a bit of a golden boy. Top of the class in all his subjects, a great sportsman, a talented musician, an accomplished dressmaker...' He paused, waiting for the expected ripple of laughter. 'I kid you not. Really, I had more than enough reasons to dislike him, but however much I tried, and believe me, I tried, I just couldn't do anything more than love Jimmy, in a very manly way, you understand.'

I could see Jimmy joining in with the laughter, enjoying his moment amongst the people who knew and loved him best. I felt humbled to be part of this day. Over the last ten days, I'd got to know Jimmy, the man behind the public façade, but being here today gave me an even deeper insight into his huge and warm personality.

Even so, I was relieved when the service was over and we could all file out into the sunshine. I felt someone grab hold of my wrist.

I spun round to face Jimmy, never being so re-lieved to see anyone in my life.

'Are you okay?' he asked, concern drawn on his features.

I nodded mutely, not trusting myself to speak in earshot of the other mourners, trying hard to keep a lid on the sheer pleasure I felt at seeing him again. With a barely imperceptible tilt of my head, I indicated to Jimmy to follow me to a quiet spot be-neath the canopy of the yew tree, away from the milling crowds.

'Wasn't it a wonderful service? So touching. I thought...' Tears pricked at the back of my eyes, re-lief flooding through my bones that he was still here talking to me, swiftly followed by guilt that I was thinking only of myself. 'Oh, Jimmy!'

'What?'

'I thought you'd gone. Seeing you in the church amongst your friends, your coffin, I thought I might never see you again.'

'And here I am,' he said, holding his arms open wide, a big grin on his face as though this whole thing was a huge joke. 'You don't get rid of me that easily!' His hand touched my face. 'Come on,' he said, guiding me by the elbow through the throng.

Wandering through the crowds, I felt like a fraud. As if I was intruding on something I had no right to be involved in, like a gatecrasher at a party. I hung back, trying to blend in with the old stone walls of the church, but Jimmy wasn't having any of that.

'There's someone I want you to meet.'

'Don't be silly,' I muttered, beneath my breath. What was he thinking? It wasn't as if he could exactly introduce me to anyone. My eyes scanned the unfamiliar faces. People were milling, chatting, their shock almost palpable. And then the crowds suddenly cleared and we came to a halt and I found myself, self-conscious and blushing, in front of Jimmy's mum and dad.

'Hello, dear,' she said, brandishing a smile every bit as bright and wide as her son's, as she took my hand in hers. 'Thank you so much for coming. Jimmy would have been so thrilled to see so many friendly faces here.'

'Yes, wouldn't he? I'm sure he's here somewhere

overseeing it all, wondering what all the fuss is about.'

She threw back her head and laughed, the sadness in her eyes lifting for a moment.

'I said exactly the same thing to Michael.' Her husband squeezed her shoulder and gave me a warm smile. 'When we were in the church, I experienced the most peculiar sensation. An overwhelming sense of peace and harmony came over me. I'm sure Jimmy was there at my side, telling me that everything would be okay. I know that sounds ridiculous, but it's absolutely true.'

'No, not at all!' I only wished I could tell her the truth. That Jimmy had indeed been at her side, but they would all have laughed me out of the church.

'Jimmy loved a good do. Were you a friend of his...?'

'Yes,' I said, momentarily taken aback. 'I knew Jimmy from London. We'd only recently got to know each other, but we were...' I faltered.

'Good friends,' Jimmy whispered in my ear.

'Good friends,' I repeated, smiling wryly, sadness filling my heart. 'I'm Alice. Alice Fletcher. I'm so pleased I could be here today, to be part of this.'

'Yes, it was a marvellous service, wasn't it?' She paused, a heavy silence filling the air, her eyes moist with tears. 'Are you coming to the pub for a drink and a bite to eat?'

Jimmy took my arm and shook his head.

'No, I won't, thank you.' It felt rude to be saying no, but Jimmy was very insistent when he wanted to be. 'I'm sure you'll struggle to get all these people in as it is, and I really must get back.'

'Of course. Well, we're very grateful to you for coming, aren't we, Michael? And if you're ever up this way, then you must promise to pop in and see us. You know where we live, don't you? Honeysuckle Cottage on the village green. You can't miss us.'

'Thank you. I'd like that.'

I felt a pang of regret for chatting with Jimmy's parents so very briefly, our paths crossing fleetingly, knowing that, in reality, we probably wouldn't meet up again. Why would we, without Jimmy being around? And yet here he was beside me, tugging at my hand, urging me to get a move on, playing an ever-increasing role in my life.

'Bye,' I said, the word catching in the back of my throat.

She didn't hear me. Rosemary and Michael had moved on, greeting the next group of people who'd come to pay their respects to their son, and I was able to slip away, following Jimmy through the shadows of the churchyard.

8

'What are you doing in there?'

'I'll be out in a minute,' I called, from the other side of the bedroom door, sinking dejectedly onto the bed. Not only did I have to find something suitable to wear from the pile of rags on my bed, but I then I had to go and face my very discerning house guest, who had an unnerving habit of hovering with intent. Now I knew why I enjoyed the single life so much. Not having to worry about anybody's opinion but my own. I threw on my jeans and long tunic top in an exotic floral print, rejected earlier because they were far too casual, but in the absence of anything better, I deemed them perfect for a night in the pub.

'Alice, come out! I'm getting very bored out here.'

Quickly, I applied a lick of mascara, a brush of bronzer and a smearing of lip gloss and opened the bedroom door.

'Whoa, look at you!' Jimmy reeled backwards from the door, taking in my appearance. 'Very nice,' he said appraisingly.

'Thanks,' I said, blushing.

'I thought I'd do us a stir fry. Will only take a few minutes and then we can settle down and watch *I'm a Celebrity*. Personally, I can't see why anyone would put themselves through the humiliation of being on that show, but I know a couple of the people on it tonight, so it should be good for a laugh. Oh, and I picked up some of your favourites!' He held up a couple of shiny bags of chocolates to tempt me.

I shook my head, smiling indulgently. The apparent ease with which Jimmy seemed able to source all manner of things – chocolate, wine, specialist cheeses – was something of a worry.

'Where did you get those?'

'Don't worry about it. My treat. It's really quite easy to get hold of things here if you know how.'

'Jimmy? Please don't tell me you stole them.'

'Alice, really! What do you take me for? A common thief? No, I didn't steal them. I just did a bit of judicious stocktaking down at the local supermarket. No one's any the wiser!'

'That is shocking, Jimmy,' I said, laughing. 'Really, what would your legion of fans say if they knew?'

'Ah well, that just goes to show how circumstances change. One day I'm a highly successful TV presenter, the next I'm an impoverished ghost. Needs must and all that. But don't worry, no one will be held accountable. All the paperwork is present and correct!'

'Well. Thank you. I think. I'll save them for later, if you don't mind.'

'Ah right, of course.' Jimmy's grey eyes narrowed and his shoulders slumped as he looked me up and down again in that way that did funny things to my insides.

'You're out tonight, aren't you? I'd completely

forgotten.' His tone was light, but his disappoint-ment was palpable and I don't know if it was the way he looked at me or the promise of that stir fry, but I realised the last thing I wanted to do was to go out and leave him behind.

Thinking about it, after the emotional trauma of yesterday's funeral, I was being heartless even considering it. I was his only friend in the world and my priority had to be looking after him. There'd be plenty of time for socialising after he'd left. That was if he ever left.

I peeled off my jacket and hung it over the back of a chair.

'Well, I was meant to be,' I said, trying to make it sound as though it was no big deal, 'but to be honest, I really don't fancy it now.' I was sure Damon would understand. There'd be loads of people at his leaving do and it would be unlikely he'd even notice I was missing. I'd text him later to explain. 'The offer of dinner and a night in front of the box sounds much more appealing.'

'No. Don't go changing your plans on my ac-count. You look stunning, you should go out and enjoy yourself. I'll be fine here on my own. I might even look up a few old friends.'

'That settles it, then,' I said laughing. 'I'm definitely not going out now. I don't think you should wander too far from home. It might not be safe out there and it might muck up our plans to get you over to the other side.'

I looked across at the dining table. It had been laid with a heavy white linen cloth, a candle was flickering at the centre and with the lights dimmed, it created a mellow, romantic atmosphere.

'Besides,' I added, 'tonight will be the perfect opportunity.'

'A perfect opportunity for what?'

'To have a séance! You've been here for over a couple of weeks now, Jimmy, and still there's no sign of you being moved over. I'm worried that the longer it goes on the harder it will be to make the transition. Let's ask the spirits for help. I've had a look on the internet, it all seems quite straightforward. And if anyone can give us some answers, it will be them.'

Jimmy frowned, giving me a scathing look.

'Absolutely not, Alice. Promise me you'll never

try that. Don't you know how dangerous those things can be? We might make contact with the wrong type of spirits entirely and get ourselves into a whole heap of trouble. You don't know what you're messing with.' He stormed over to the fridge, yanked open the door and pulled out some vegetables. 'Are you really that desperate to get rid of me?'

'No, it isn't that, Jimmy. You can stay for as long as it takes.' I paused, looking across at him, his arms laden with food, my heart tugging at the hurt expression on his face. 'I love having you here and, heaven knows, it will be so quiet and lonely when you're gone, but I know that you don't really belong here. This isn't fair on you. Aren't you desperate to get wherever it is you should be going?'

He shrugged, the corners of his mouth twisting in a smile.

'I don't know, I quite like it here,' he said softly. He released the ingredients in his arms onto the worktop and wandered over to where I was standing. He stood opposite me, and grabbed my arms, his gaze penetrating my face.

'I'm sorry. I know it must seem as though I'm not being very proactive in getting myself out of your hair, but that's only because I don't believe there's anything I can do. I don't think it's one of those things you can force. Don't ask me how I know that. It's just something I feel inside here.'

He tapped his heart with his fist, his sincerity shining through.

'I think, when the time is right, I'll be taken across, regardless of anything you or I might be doing. And I honestly don't think it will take that long. A couple of weeks at the most. Do you think you can put up with me until then?'

'Of course I can. It's not about that. It's just that I feel responsible for you. It's as though I've been handed this task of looking after you, of making sure you get to your spiritual home, and I feel completely frustrated that I'm unable to live up to that task. I feel like a failure, if you must know. If I'd been at work, I'd have probably been sacked by now.'

'Nonsense,' he said with a smile, stroking my hair away from my face. He was so close I could smell his masculine scent, see the pores of his skin and feel his breath on my face. The air between us sizzled with electricity. 'You've been doing a brilliant job at looking after me. I'll tell you something, some of the five-star hotels I've stayed in haven't been half as good as this place. And it's not as though you haven't tried getting rid of me. That ceremony in the field with that irate farmer was inspired! Why it didn't work I have no idea!'

'Would you stop it!' I felt my face flush with heat at the memory. Or was it from the close proximity of Jimmy? I wasn't sure. I only knew my stomach was tense with anxiety and desire. I didn't want to admit to Jimmy just how much he had come to mean to me in such a short space of time. He had enough to think about without worrying about me and the silly crush I was nursing. Being a TV star, I guessed he was used to that kind of attention, but in his current predicament, I was certain it was the last thing he needed. I sighed and gave a rueful shrug. 'I'll never live that one down, will I?'

'Well, at least I'll go to my final resting place with a big smile on my face.' My stomach plummeted, I hated it when he joked about this whole thing.

'Come on,' he said, putting an arm around my shoulder. 'Don't look like that.'

My eyes closed and my entire body fired with the closeness of his touch, before he abruptly pulled away. His gaze lingered on my face and I wondered if I'd imagined the flash of desire stirring in his eyes. 'I should get the dinner started,' he said, quietly.

As he turned away, leaving me with my arms aching with emptiness, my gaze flickered over at the table. The séance had been a rotten idea. A romantic dinner for two sounded much, much better.

9

Banging on my front door early on a Sunday morning could only mean one thing.

'Lexie, can you not sleep?' I said, grumpily, tying my towelling robe around me, and ushering her inside.

'Clean living, that's me. Early to bed, early to rise.' She breezed past me, her eyes doing a quick scan of every nook and cranny of my small flat, before turning to give my dishevelled figure a cursory up and down. 'Obviously, the same can't be said for you,' she said, looking at me suspiciously.

'Can't I even have a lie-in now? It is the weekend!' She was beginning to make a habit of this, checking up on my movements. I wandered out into the kitchen, filled the kettle with water and flicked it on. Jimmy wafted in and helped himself to a grape from the fruit bowl.

'You know, your sister can be a real pain in the butt at times, can't she?'

That was all I needed. Jimmy putting his oar in.

'No, you can't,' she said, forcefully. 'Not until you tell me what you're up to. You've been acting odd for weeks now. And what's all this nonsense about you going off to some aunt's funeral? Which aunt of ours would that be?' she asked, arching an eyebrow.

I dropped my gaze from her accusatory stare, my mind darting in all directions for an answer.

'I spoke to your office on Friday,' she went on. 'So unless you didn't want to burden me with the tragic news of the death of our beloved relative, I suspect you either had a job interview or you were up to something illicit with someone highly unsuitable. I do hope it's the latter,' she said, with undisguised glee.

I gave her a withering glance and Jimmy one

too, for good measure, because he was looking at me expectantly, waiting for my response. I could so do without all this this morning.

'Well, sorry to disappoint you.' I shuffled around the kitchen, pulling mugs from cupboards. 'But it was neither of those things. I did go to a funeral, if you must know. Not an aunt's, obviously, but a friend's. I didn't want to make a big thing of it at work, that's all.'

Lexie didn't look disappointed, just amazed. Her eyes had grown wide and her mouth gaped open.

'A friend? No, really? That's terrible. Which friend? Why didn't you say anything?'

I sighed and handed her a steaming mug, trying to avoid Jimmy's gaze. Clearly, Lexie wasn't going to drop the subject and Jimmy's ghostly presence was doing nothing to help my squirming discomfort.

'It was no one you knew, just someone I...'

'Alice, come on, stop messing me around. Just tell me who it was.'

I was going to get so much ribbing over this, I just knew it.

'Jimmy,' I said quietly into the collar of my

dressing gown as I picked off an imaginary thread from the arm.

'Jimmy? Who the hell was Jimmy?'

I sat down at the kitchen table, sighing, and folded my arms defensively.

'Jimmy Mack,' I said, my gaze drifting over to the man himself.

'What?' Her mouth curled up in disbelief. 'Jimmy Mack? You went to his funeral? What on earth for?'

Now there was a question. How could I possibly explain to Lexie? And even if I did, would she ever believe such a far-fetched story? It was all such a mess, and really I had no idea how to get myself out of it.

'I just felt as if I wanted to,' I said with growing conviction. 'When I heard he'd died, I felt a connection with him. A loss, I suppose.' In the background, Jimmy nodded approvingly. 'He's been so much a part of our lives, we practically grew up watching him on the telly.'

'Ouch, that makes me feel really ancient,' grumbled Jimmy.

'I wanted to say my goodbyes to him, that was all.'

Inwardly, I glowed with satisfaction, thinking I'd handled the whole thing really rather well, but Lexie was looking at me as if I'd suddenly grown a second head.

'Well that is terribly sad,' she said, a tad dramatically.

'I know, it was, wasn't it? I was so upset when I found out the news, I...'

'No, not sad sad, but pathetic sad. You really must get out more, Alice, make some new friends.' Lexie tilted her head, adopting a pitying expression. 'You clearly haven't got enough going on in your life if you feel the need to go to some celebrity has-been's funeral.'

'Bloody cheek!' said Jimmy, folding his arms crossly.

I gave him a reassuring shrug of my shoulders, out of Lexie's line of vision, and listened as she continued on her rant.

'Haven't you got anything better to do with your time?'

'He wasn't a has-been.' I felt duty bound to correct her, with Jimmy looking increasingly disgruntled. 'I'm sure lots of people feel the same way as I do. He's left a huge gap. I know he'll be sorely missed.'

'You reckon? Hmm, I'm not so sure about that now.' She dropped the day's papers on my coffee table, a look of triumph on her face. 'Didn't I say there'd be something fishy behind all this? I don't think your Mr Mack was such a gentleman after all.'

'What do you mean?' Both Jimmy and I leant over the table, craning to read the headline.

Exclusive: Jimmy Mack's secret lover, the mother of his unborn child, revealed!

'It can't be true!' My fingers tore through the pages to the double-page centre spread.

A picture of reality TV star Donna Diamond, with her peroxide blonde hair and surgically enhanced chest, leapt off the page.

Read about my passionate nights with sex-crazed Jimmy Mack.

'I don't believe it!' I cried, as my eyes struggled to make sense of the words.

'Shit, no!' said Jimmy, burying his head in his hands. He rubbed his scalp furiously as Lexie read out the juiciest snippets.

Jimmy was a voracious lover. He was unlike any man I'd ever met before.

'Oo-er.' Lexie helpfully filled in the appropriate sound effects.

We were soulmates

'Oooh!'

Our plans to marry devastated by his premature death.

'Aahh.'

I'll always have a part of him in our unborn child.

'Sob.'

Lexie rolled her eyes dismissively, pushing the newspaper aside.

'So, Mr Squeaky Clean didn't lead such a blameless life as he'd have us believe, eh? Who'd have thought it? Him and Donna Diamond. A most unlikely couple, don't you think?'

My mouth opened, but the words caught at the back of my throat.

'Was she there?' Lexie asked.

My mind was awash with all sorts of thoughts and feelings. My throat was dry and I felt sick, unable to even look at Jimmy. And what was that other peculiar feeling? The gut-stirring emotion in the pit of my stomach. I paced up and down the living room, my arms hugging my middle.

Betrayed, that was it. I felt betrayed. What was that all about? Jimmy had played no part in my life when he'd been alive, so I had no reason to feel hard done by now, but I did. I felt I'd come to know the real Jimmy Mack, sweet and gentle and funny, but here in black and white I was confronted with a totally different version of the man who was taking up so much of my head space.

'Is it true?' I asked, looking across at Jimmy, totally forgetting Lexie's presence.

'What? Of course it's true. It says it here, doesn't it?' said Lexie. She'd always loved a bit of gossip. 'So was she there, at the funeral?'

'What? No. No, she wasn't.' From the little I knew of Donna Diamond, she wasn't the blending into the background type. If she'd been there, we would have all known about it.

I looked across at Jimmy again, my skin fired with outrage. A dozen questions danced for attention on my tongue, none of which I could voice with Lexie in the room. Jimmy was poring over the paper, shaking his head, his skin turning an unbecoming grey even for a ghost.

'No, of course it isn't true,' he said, looking affronted. He stood up, sighing heavily, and walked over to the window, resting his hand on the ledge as he gazed out at the city below. 'Unless, of course, it was an immaculate conception. I mean, I don't even know the woman. We sat together at some charity luncheon a few months ago, that's all.'

He looked totally defeated and vulnerable standing there, and my heart ached for him. I wandered over to the window, longing to touch him, but aware that Lexie was watching me all the time. Why would Donna Diamond be so cruel as to make up something so damning and awful?

'Are you all right?' asked Lexie, eyeing me warily. 'I honestly didn't realise you were such a fan of the bloke, but this sort of thing, well, you'd kind of expect it, wouldn't you?'

'No,' I said, sounding suitably outraged.

'No!' cried Jimmy, echoing my sentiment.

'Okay, okay,' said Lexie huffily, folding her arms across her chest. 'I'm sorry, but it's not my fault if the object of your affections was a player.' She folded up the paper and put it to one side. 'Really, though, Alice, maybe you should think about finding someone new and, um, alive and kicking, you know, someone you can have a proper relationship with.'

Clearly, my sister thought I was emotionally unhinged, and why wouldn't she? But that wasn't my concern right now. Jimmy looked crushed, all his energy had deserted him and I desperately needed to comfort him. There was no chance of doing that with Lexie around.

'There is something I need to talk to you about, Lexie. Men problems.' I sighed dramatically, as though I had a whole list of them. 'But not now. I've got one hell of a migraine and I'm going back to bed. How about we get together in the week for a glass of wine and a chat? I could do with some advice. Can we get together one night next week? How about Wednesday?'

Both Lexie and Jimmy looked at me, wide-eyed and doubtful, as though I'd suggested I might join a nunnery.

'Great,' said Lexie, standing up and fastening the buttons on her jacket. 'Wednesday it is, then.'

* * *

Hurrying back into the living room, I found Jimmy sitting at my pine table, his shoulders hunched over the paper. My heart bled for him.

'Don't even bother reading it, Jimmy. You'll only

upset yourself. What is it they say? Today's newspapers are tomorrow's fish wrapping.'

He turned his head and looked up at me, his deep-set grey eyes brimming with emotion.

'They say a lot of things. There's no smoke without fire. Mud sticks. Dead men don't tell lies. The thing is, I have no way of defending myself against this sort of thing.' He shook his head, pushing the paper away in frustration. 'What on earth will my parents and friends think?'

I placed my arm around his shoulder and ran my fingers through his dark, thick hair. It seemed the most natural thing in the world to do, but it didn't stop me from having a pinch me 'I'm fondling Jimmy Mack' moment.

'Try not to worry about it,' I said, not entirely convincingly, still uncertain of the truth. 'They know the real you, the person you are. It won't change their memories of you. All this, well, of course it's a shock, but it doesn't really change anything.'

He snorted derisively.

'Alice, it changes everything. It's more important now than if I were still alive. At least then I'd have the chance to give my side of the story, but what chance have I got now? This woman, well, she can just ruin me with her lies.'

I hated seeing him like this. His life, or afterlife, whatever you liked to call it, was frustrating enough as it was, stuck with only me as a companion in my pokey little flat, but having near strangers make up outrageous lies about you, it was downright unfair. What I still couldn't understand was why Donna Diamond would go to all that trouble if there was no truth in the story. And, however much I wanted to believe Jimmy, I knew I wouldn't be happy until I'd satisfied myself that he was being totally honest about all of this.

'Look, are you absolutely certain that nothing happened between you and Donna? A one-night stand, maybe? It happens all the time. Perhaps you'd had too much to drink and can't remember the details. Umm...' My voice trailed away as I noticed Jimmy's thunderous expression.

'What, you think I'd forget a shag with a pneumatic blonde bombshell? Well, thanks very much for the character reference. No, Alice, there was no one-night stand, not even a chaste kiss. Believe me, I would have remembered that. Have you seen the woman? She'd have eaten me up and spat me out for breakfast.'

I giggled. Come to think of it, it was a huge leap of the imagination.

'Sorry, it's just hard to believe anyone could do that sort of thing.'

'Welcome to the wonderful world of television. She's looking for her fifteen minutes of fame, a book deal, TV interviews, and with me off the scene she thinks she's found the ideal opportunity. Hey, it's a great career move. For her.'

'But how can she live with herself? And what about the poor baby?'

'That's if there is one,' Jimmy added bitterly.

I sighed, realising the world Jimmy came from was a million miles away from the world I inhabited. I wished there was something I could do for him.

'Well, she can't be allowed to get away with it,' I said, feeling anger stirring in my bones. 'It's totally wrong. Can't you go and sort her out? Have a quiet word or something?'

He chuckled, the sound of his laughter reminding me reassuringly of the Jimmy I'd come to know in recent days.

'You're so funny, Alice. I think that might be an abuse of my limited powers. No,' he sighed, stretching his arms high above his head, 'there's nothing I can do.'

I slumped back down in my seat, a heavy silence filling the space between us as we both mulled over this latest turn of events. Then, with a start, Jimmy jumped up from his chair and slapped me on the leg.

'Don't you see, this all makes perfect sense now! Didn't we say there had to be a reason why I'm stuck here?'

'Yes, but what's that possibly got to do with this?' I asked, perplexed, holding up the offending newspaper.

'Well, this is obviously it, why I've been kept here, to sort out all this mess in the papers. I can't go to my resting place knowing all these lies are circulating about me. It wouldn't be right. There's a new life coming into the world and that baby has the right to know its true parentage. If I can put the truth out there, then that's when I'll be able to pass over peacefully.'

'Do you really think so?' I looked up into Jimmy's eyes, seeing the hope there. 'Do you think it's some sort of initiation task, then? Complete this and then you can come on over.'

Jimmy laughed, shaking his head.

'No, I don't think it's an entrance exam for heaven, if that's what you mean,' he said, chastising me with a look. 'I think it's free entry for all, but clearly I've got an opportunity to sort out this mess. Once it's all untangled, I'll bet you anything I'll be out of here and on my way to the top floor before you know it.'

'I suppose it makes sense in a weird kind of way,' I said, not really appreciating his flippant manner.

'It makes absolute sense, Alice.'

'But how on earth are you going to do that? It's hardly as if you can go and speak to Donna and reason with her. Can you? I mean, have you tried?'

'I know. I can't seem to get through to anyone but you, Alice.' He paused, a smile hovering on his lips as his eyes looked at me beseechingly. 'There's nothing I can do, but there's nothing preventing you from going to see Donna. You could speak to her, explain the situation.'

'Ha ha,' I laughed, in a not entirely natural manner. Jimmy wasn't laughing, though, he had his ultra-serious face on.

'Really, it's the ideal solution. You must see the damage this rubbish will do to my reputation.' He ripped the paper from my hands. 'We have to do something about it. Especially now we know it's the reason why I'm stuck here. You're the only person who can help, Alice.'

'But, Jimmy, I don't even know the woman. She's hardly likely to listen to me, a lowly PA. And it's not as if I can turn up and say, "Hi, you don't know me, but I'm best mates with the ghost of Jimmy Mack and he'd really appreciate it if you'd stop spreading filthy lies about him." She'd laugh in my face.'

My whole body sighed with exhaustion. Being entirely responsible for the physical and emotional wellbeing of a left-out-in-the-cold ghost was a huge burden.

Jimmy's eyes narrowed as he chewed on the inside of his lip.

'Are you saying you won't help me then?' The grey eyes were giving me the full-on guilt trip treatment again. 'You know I can't stay here forever. You said yourself, we have to find a way of getting me sent over to the other side, and then when we do find a possible solution, you're not prepared to help.'

'Please, don't be like that. It's not that I don't want to help, but really, think about it, what can I do?'

He sank to his knees on the floor in front of me and clutched my wrists with his hands, looking up at me imploringly.

'I know it's a lot to ask of you, Alice. After everything else you've done for me. And I wouldn't ask if I didn't have to. But I'm begging you, Alice, I really need you to do this one thing for me. I have to clear my name. I have to move on. And you're the only person who can help me to do that.'

Looking down into his deep-set eyes, boring into my soul, I sighed heavily.

Please God. Your spiritual highness. Heavenly master of all things ghostly. Anyone. Please. Help me. Do something, anything to sort out this unholy mess.

I waited. And then waited a little more. There was no response from any of those higher heavenly authorities.

'Of course I'll help you,' I said, smiling weakly.

10

If I'd hoped that the furore surrounding the revelations about Jimmy's love life might have settled down after a few days, then I was very much mistaken.

By Tuesday morning, most of the papers were running articles probing into the personal life of Jimmy Mack; his ex-girlfriends, his lifestyle, one even questioned his sexuality, but most focused on his doomed relationship with Donna. 'Had Jimmy found true love at last?' screamed a headline.

'No, he bloody well hadn't!' was Jimmy's emphatic response to that one.

Ordinarily, I'd have been as enthralled as the

next person flicking through the paper with some spare time on their hands, but with a disgruntled spook looking over my shoulder, I had to at least pretend to be disinterested.

'There are some lovely photos of you here, though,' I said brightly. 'Look.'

'Honestly, Alice, is that supposed to make me feel better? A few poxy photos. By running this story, they're ruining my reputation. Lord knows it would have been so easy to go out with a whole string of these girls.' He stabbed a dismissive finger at a photo of Donna Diamond. 'But I deliberately kept away from that whole party scene. I didn't want to be part of a celebrity couple, opening my personal life up to the magazines in the way some people do. I wanted something more than that. Something real. I was holding out for that. I told you that, didn't I?' His voice drifted away and I could hear the frustration colouring his words.

'I know,' I said, clutching my arms around my waist. 'I know.'

He held my gaze, looking at me imploringly. A heat rose in my cheeks.

'Look.' He scrabbled around in his trouser

pocket and pulled out a scrap of paper. 'I've got all her details here, phone numbers, address, email. You can contact her, yeah? Talk to her. Make her see sense.' A light shone in his eyes: excitement, hope or something else – I couldn't be sure. But I knew one thing. I couldn't be the person to dampen that light. I had to be one to make sure that the light kept shining for as long as Jimmy was at my side.

* * *

A lot of my conversations had turned into the difficult variety over these last few weeks, but tonight's with Lexie would be taking the difficult conversation scenario to a whole new level.

Thankfully, the pizzeria was buzzing for a weekday evening. It meant we could talk without being overheard. The sort of stuff I had to raise with Lexie wasn't the sort of thing you wanted tripping off the tongues of the locals and echoing down the High Street.

'So come on,' she said, as soon as we were tucking into our bowls of Spaghetti alle Vongole, 'what's this all about, Alice? I've been dying to know.'

'Well...' I picked up the wine bottle from the middle of the table and topped up our glasses. 'It's a bit delicate, actually.'

She dropped her head to one side, her expression a mix of concern and bewilderment.

'Oh, come on, Alice, whatever it is, you know you can tell me. I'm unshockable.'

'Well...' I started again. Perhaps if I blurted it all out quickly, it might seem remotely believable. 'You know all that business about Jimmy Mack and—'

Lexie interrupted before I had a chance to explain.

'You're not still going on about him? That's old news, Alice.' She reached across and grabbed my wrist, a look of concern upon her face. 'Really, Alice, do you not think you're taking this whole thing a bit too seriously? I know you liked the guy, but you're in danger of becoming obsessive about him.'

'No,' I pleaded. 'You don't understand. I...'

'You're right there.' She leant back in her chair, giving me a doubtful look. 'I don't understand.'

We sat in silence for a few moments, eyeing each other warily, before I took a deep breath.

'It's just that I know for a fact that all that rubbish Donna Diamond is spouting in the papers about her relationship with Jimmy is simply not true. She's not carrying his baby, it's all a load of lies.'

'But how can you possibly—?'

Now it was my turn to interrupt. I held up my hand to stop her.

'I know, Lexie. Trust me. And I know too how much all the gossip and lies are hurting Jimmy, damaging his memory.'

'Okay, I can accept that it might not be true, but what I can't understand is why you're so upset about it. I mean, what's it to you? It wasn't as if you were a huge fan of his when he was alive.'

I sighed inwardly. How could Lexie possibly understand? If I'd been in her shoes, I would have felt equally puzzled by such erratic behaviour.

'The thing is,' I said, leaning over the table conspiratorially, 'I have a connection with Jimmy.'

Lexie's fork stopped in mid-air, her eyes

growing wide. Great. Now I had her full and undivided attention.

'You know,' I went on, 'a spiritual connection. I talk to Jimmy.'

'What the...?' exclaimed my sister, dropping her fork into the pasta bowl. 'This has gone way too far, darling. You need some help. You're obviously depressed or something. Too much time spent alone, probably. Don't worry, sweetie,' she said, her fingers interlocking with mine over the table. 'We're going to get some help for you, get you properly sorted.'

I yanked my hand away, sitting up crossly.

'I'm not depressed, and I don't need help. Well, not the sort of help you're suggesting, anyway. I know it's hard to believe and I'm not quite sure how it's happened and I really wish it hadn't happened, but I am in contact with Jimmy and I've made a promise to him. And I'm determined to keep that promise. I hoped you might help me, but if you won't, then I'll have to sort it out for myself.'

Lexie nodded, adopting an uncharacteristically sympathetic expression. One you might use on the realisation that you're in the company of a mentally unhinged person. She shifted uneasily in her chair.

'So, um, do you hear voices, then?' she ventured.

'No, not voices. Just Jimmy's voice.'

'Ah, I see.'

'No, you don't see, Lexie. I'm not on the verge of some mental breakdown if that's what you're thinking.'

'Okay, but help me out here, Alice. It's all sounding a bit freaky from where I'm standing. You speak to Jimmy Mack? A dead man. How does that work?'

Relief rushed through my bones. It felt wonderful to be able to say the words out loud, even if Lexie was looking at me as though I'd completely lost the plot. Maybe, just maybe, she would be able to make a difference. For me and for Jimmy. For weeks, I'd hugged this huge secret to myself, not knowing which way to turn, and now I had the chance to share it with my sister. She would help, wouldn't she?

'I know it sounds freaky, but it isn't really.' I shuffled my chair closer to the table. 'Not when you get used to the idea. I met Jimmy the day he died. He'd had an accident. In his car.' I giggled at the ridiculousness of my words. 'Well, of course he'd had an accident, everyone knows that now, only I didn't know he was dead at the time. I mean, it's not the sort of thing you normally think about when you meet someone for the first time, is it? You sort of take it for granted that they're alive. Obviously that bit came as a shock, finding out he was dead.'

'Obviously,' she said, nodding her head slowly.

'Only when I got talking to him and got to know him better, I soon forgot that he was dead.'

'Right. Yes. I can see how you might.'

I paused for breath, taking another mouthful of wine. I looked across at Lexie, who was gawping at me like a stunned rabbit, all doe-eyed and vulnerable. Her mouth gaped open and shut, as if she was about to say something, but when nothing was forthcoming, I continued.

'The thing is, there was a bit of a problem with Jimmy moving over to the other side.' Lexie's startled gaze followed my finger as it pointed upwards. 'We couldn't think why he'd got stuck here with me, it didn't make any sense, but obviously I said he could stay until we found a way to move him over.'

'Jimmy is staying at your flat?' she said in a barely recognisable voice.

'Yes.' I nodded wildly. 'And then when we found out that Donna Diamond was spreading all those awful lies about him, well, everything fell into place. Jimmy has to clear his name, that's what this is all about. It's obvious that he needs to sort out this horrible business with Donna before he'll be allowed to move over. The trouble is, he can't do that on his own. I've been chosen to help him. When I saw how upset Jimmy was about the whole thing, I agreed to go and see Donna. We have to make her retract her statement.'

'We?'

'Yes. You and me. You have to help me, Lexie? There isn't anyone else I can ask. Please?'

Distractedly, I waved away the waitress who'd arrived bearing dessert menus, my eyes gazing imploringly at Lexie.

'Please tell me this is a wind-up,' she asked hopefully. 'Some kind of a joke. Ha ha. Very funny.' She didn't look the remotest bit amused, though.

'It's no joke!' I said, exasperated. It was impossible. What on earth could I do to make Lexie understand?

A prickly silence hung over us, and I was beginning to think that this whole idea had been stupid and we should both go home and try to forget that we had ever had this frankly weird conversation, when a familiar scent wafted past my nose. Musky, woody and very masculine.

'Jimmy!' I never thought I'd be so pleased to see my ghostly housemate. He pulled out a chair from the next table and placed it in between Lexie and me. Her chin hit the floor as her gaze followed the approaching chair, complete incomprehension painting her features. I flung an arm out and made a show of wiggling the chair back and forth for the benefit of the curious stares from the other diners, grinning like a demented ghost whisperer all the time.

'Oh, Jimmy,' I breathed, dropping my head into my hands. 'I'm really sorry. I know I shouldn't have said anything, but I didn't know what else to do. I just can't cope with this on my own any more and I thought Lexie might be able to help.' I shook my head ruefully, thinking I'd made a big mistake.

Lexie clearly thought I was way past helping, the way she was gawping at me.

'Hey, don't worry about it,' Jimmy said, leaning over and kissing my cheek lightly. I felt my cheeks flush with warmth. It must have had something to do with his heavenly status, but every time he touched me, it sent electrifying shivers rippling through my body. I was simply relieved he wasn't cross with me. I felt certain I'd breached some spiritual regulation by offloading my secret.

Lexie's eyes were wide as she looked from me to the chair, then she coughed, clearing her throat.

'Are you, um, talking to your friend now?' She loaded the words with such mistrust and scepticism I half expected the men in white coats to appear from out of the woodwork.

'Yes, Lexie. Now do you believe me? Jimmy's here with us now.'

'Pleased to meet you. Formally, that is,' said Jimmy nodding in her direction. I giggled, looking between them both.

'What's so funny?'

'Jimmy's just said hello to you,' I said, sitting back in my chair and smiling smugly.

'Huh, if that's the case, then why can't I see or hear him?'

'I don't know!' I buried my head in my hands. I wanted to scream. To throw myself on the floor and kick my legs in the air, but I knew that would be a step too far, even for Lexie. But how the hell did I know why I was seemingly the only person in the world who could see and hear Jimmy?

'I don't know what's going on, Alice, but all this attention-seeking behaviour, it's really not very funny any more.'

Just then, Jimmy leant over the other way, blew in Lexie's ear and picked up her hand, planting a very gallant kiss on her fingertips.

'What the...' she yelped, swatting away an imaginary fly, 'what the hell was that?'

I burst into peals of laughter. Thank goodness for that. It was awful, but looking at Lexie jumping around in her seat, panic on her face, made me feel so much better and I felt the relief flooding through my bones.

'That was Jimmy,' I explained, still laughing. 'Don't worry about it, though. Once you get to know him, you'll see what a great guy he really is.'

* * *

'Where is he now?' Lexie had adopted a twitch and a pale expression. She kept looking furtively over each shoulder, shivering exaggeratedly.

We'd come back to my flat for a nightcap, as she was in no fit state to go home. She'd gone all shivery and shaky like the heroine in a badly made horror movie and was sitting on my sofa, her arms hugging her knees into her chest. It made me smile, seeing her so uncharacteristically lost for words, but then I remembered the bewilderment I'd felt when I first found out a ghost had become my new best friend. That sort of news takes some getting used to.

'It's all right, he's sitting over there in the armchair.' Jimmy gave a friendly wave from across the room as he helped himself to some nachos from a bowl.

'You have to be kidding me,' she exclaimed, her eyes alighting on the diminishing stack of crisps. 'Well, just as long as he stays over there, please. And can you tell him not to do the whole creeping up on me thing? That's seriously freaky.'

'Okay,' I said, gravely, shooting Jimmy a warning

look. If we wanted Lexie to help, then we needed to keep her on side. At least I had the benefit of seeing Jimmy and being able to talk to him. Even after just a short while, I'd stopped thinking of him as some weird being from another place, he was simply the man who shared my life, with all that that entailed, plus a few added complications to make things even more interesting.

For Lexie, he was just a light wisp of air and the subject of my inane mutterings. No wonder she was freaked out.

'So how long is he planning on staying for?' She looked at me warily from over the top of her mug of coffee.

'Well, that's the thing, we don't know. Obviously there's a reason why he hasn't been able to make his journey over to the other side, some reason why he's stuck here with me. But we didn't know what that was until now.'

I sighed. Talking about it with someone other than Jimmy for the first time brought home to me what an insurmountable problem I had on my hands.

'We investigated a couple of options for getting him moved on, but none of them worked.'

'Ha, ha! Tell her about the tractor. That was bloody hilarious.'

'We thought at first it might be a case of just waiting for the right moment,' I said, completely ignoring Jimmy's quip.

'I see. And you want me to help you get rid of him? Exorcise him, kind of thing.'

'Whoa!' Jimmy jumped up, making the sign of a cross with his fingers towards Lexie. 'I'm not sure I like your sister's approach.'

I giggled.

'I don't think we need to do anything quite so drastic. When all this stuff with Donna appeared in the paper, that's when we realised why he's got stuck here. She can't be allowed to get away with such blatant lies. It's really hurtful to Jimmy. They didn't even sleep together.'

'Bitch,' Lexie said, with feeling.

'Right on!' agreed Jimmy.

'Exactly!' I added. 'Jimmy's managed to get hold of her contact details, so I thought we could ring her and arrange to meet her.'

'And you really think she's going to agree to meet up with us when she has no idea who we are or what we want? Why should she when there's nothing in it for her? I should imagine she won't do anything without demanding a fee upfront.'

'She has a point,' offered Jimmy.

'No, what we need to do is run into her at one of her regular hang-outs. Make it seem like a chance meeting. That way, we can take her unawares, she won't have a chance to come up with any excuses when we confront her with the truth.'

I beamed. Everything seemed so much more manageable with Lexie on the case.

'So does that mean you'll help me?' I asked, already knowing the answer.

Lexie sighed, shaking her head wryly.

'It doesn't look as though I've got much choice in the matter, does it?'

11

'Would you hang on a moment, I can barely walk in these things, let alone run!'

Lexie and I were running, or rather tottering in my case, down the busy main road. The light rain that had started less than ten minutes ago had taken on the ferocity of a force-ten gale and my floaty skirt and skimpy top clung woefully inadequately to my body. Shivering with cold – my goosebumps had goosebumps on them – I cursed after Lexie's departing figure.

'I knew this was a bad idea. Why didn't we wait outside in the car? At least we could have kept warm and jumped out when we saw her.'

'Yes, but what if there's some sort of back entrance? You know, for the celebs. And even if she does come out the front, she's bound to have some heavy looking out for her. No, at least if we get into the club we have the opportunity of speaking to her alone.'

What had seemed like a brilliant idea a few days ago now seemed like the worst idea I'd ever had, and I'd had a few bad ones in my time.

'Eugh, I look so trashy,' I'd sighed earlier when Lexie had turned up, insisting I change out of my old faithful black trousers and jumper, taking a pair of scissors to my very old and much-loved floral maxi summer dress, transforming it into something that would have made my mother blush.

A few moments later, in my makeshift skirt, the tiniest of strappy tops and a pair of death-defying high heels, Lexie considered I was ready.

'Cinderella will go the ball,' she pronounced proudly.

'More like the ugly sister,' I said sulkily. 'Just so long as I don't bump into anyone I know. That would be embarrassing.'

Judging by the number of suspect looks and

tooting of car horns we attracted navigating the pavements, I was under no misapprehension as to how I was looking, and it wasn't demure or sweet. Trashy was definitely high up there. Now, hovering in a shop doorway, trying to find some refuge from the arctic conditions, I cursed Lexie again. My nicely straightened hair had taken on an unbecoming frizz and I was convinced I might die at any moment from hypothermia.

'Shall we forget all about this and go home? Maybe we can phone Donna and arrange an appointment to see her or send her a letter or something. Like any sensible person would.'

'Don't be silly, we're nearly there now. Come on,' she urged, grabbing me by the arm. 'We want to get in before the crowds arrive, get the best vantage point.'

Once inside, I was disappointed when Lexie refused to order me a nice warming mug of hot chocolate. Apparently they didn't do them. What kind of establishment was this? I wondered. Instead, I had to content myself with a glass of orange juice and found a seat on one of the corner leather couches, trying my best to warm up.

'It's a bit quiet, isn't it?' I said, looking around the darkened room, picking out the occasional shadowy figures.

'Well, it's early yet,' Lexie said curtly, as if I'd said something obviously stupid.

I looked at my watch. Ten-thirty wasn't early in my book.

'Can't you at least pretend to be pleased to be here? Remember, it's me that's doing you a favour. You don't want to draw attention to us, do you?'

'Sorry, Lexie.' I hated nightclubs. Hated the way my bare thighs were sticking to the oversized couch. Hated the way everyone eyed one another up, as if deciding on whether to plump for the sherry trifle or the apple pie from the dessert trolley. The whole scene made me feel uncomfortable, even more so in my ridiculous outfit.

Two hours later, the place was beginning to fill up and it was a job to make out who was who under the subdued lighting.

'Wait here,' said Lexie, 'I'll go and do a quick recce, see if I can spot Donna.'

'Okay.' I leant against a pillar, watching my sister disappear into the crowds, only slightly fearful that I might be abducted into the white slave trade.

'Hello, darling,' a deeply lecherous voice rang in my ear, 'what's a nice girl like you doing in a place like this?'

'Jimmy!' I jumped, as though I'd actually seen a ghost, but couldn't stop myself from smiling, a warm fuzzy feeling filling my insides. His cheeky expression popping up when you least expected it always lifted my spirits, but then I remembered he was the reason I was sitting in this godforsaken club in the first place.

'The things I do for you,' I said, huffily. 'I hope this is worth all the effort. You haven't seen Donna around, have you?'

'Not yet,' he grinned, helping himself to a sip of my drink, 'but I have it on good authority she'll be turning up later.'

'Really? How do you know that?'

He laughed, slipped an arm around my waist and, taking me by surprise, pulled me in tight to his body.

'Do you want to dance?' His voice came out in a

whisper, the subdued lighting adding to the intimacy of our embrace.

I glanced all around me. It always felt illicit being with Jimmy, as though we were in the midst of a secret love affair, about to be discovered, but in the dark shadows of the club, no one would notice us.

'I'd love to,' I said, laughing, wrapping my arms around his neck. My breathing quickened as my body melded against his and we swayed in time to the beat of the music. Looking up into his eyes, it was easy to imagine meeting him like this for the first time under different circumstances. Meeting him as a real live living man! How surreal would that have been? It was almost too poignant to consider.

'You have to remember I have insider information,' he said, his eyes gently mocking me.

'How? Tell me.' I banged my fist on his chest playfully. 'I need to know these things.'

'I've told you,' he said, laughing. He spun me around at arm's length, before pulling me back close to his body, which did nothing for my already giddy state. 'I visualise the person in my head, concentrate on them for a few seconds, and whoosh, I'm there. It's pretty cool.'

I gazed up at him in awe and adoration. Not only was he the most gorgeous man I had ever set my eyes on, but he could do things no other man could ever do. It was the deadliest combination.

'Cool, yes! I wish I could have a go. That would be so amazing.'

'No, really, you don't, Alice. Be careful what you wish for and all that.'

'Yeah, sorry, I wasn't thinking straight.' To be honest, it was difficult to think of anything when I was still pressed hard against his body. If this was what clubbing was all about then I could definitely get used to it.

'So we ought to hang around a while, you reckon?'

'Definitely. She'll be here in about fifteen minutes.' He sat me back down again. 'Anyway, I'm going to shoot. I only wanted to check that you were both okay. It's probably best if I don't hang around. I'll get back to the flat. But any problems, just give me a call.'

It was only after Jimmy had left that I wondered how exactly he expected me to do that. I felt deflated, all my energy and enthusiasm leaving the building along with Jimmy.

Moments later, Lexie breezed back, shaking her head.

'Nope, there's no sign of her yet. I suppose there was no guarantee she would come tonight. We might have to admit defeat and come back some other time.'

'No, she's definitely coming,' I said, taking a nonchalant sip from my drink.

Lexie raised her eyebrows questioningly. 'Really?'

'I feel it in my bones,' I added unconvincingly.

'Okay. So that means Jimmy's here then, is he?'

Rumbled. I could only shrug my shoulders.

'Well, he was here a minute ago,' I said, looking around, realising he'd already done his disappearing act. 'He reckons she's coming, but who knows? Maybe we should give it another half an hour or so then call it a night.'

'Yeah, that's not a bad idea. Wait here, I'll go and get us another drink. How about something stronger this time? You look like a Girl Guide, sitting there sipping on your orange juice.'

I laughed. Certainly, I'd have felt a lot more at home at a Girl Guides' Jamboree rather than sitting in this depressing hole, but at least I knew we'd be going home soon. The sooner the better, as far as I was concerned.

'Quick,' urged Lexie, a few minutes later, almost showering me with the contents of the wine glasses she was holding. 'It's Donna, she's arrived!'

'Has she?' I gasped, suddenly feeling panicked. I jumped up, then immediately sat down again. Maybe this wasn't such a good idea after all. What on earth would we say to her? Thankfully, I didn't have too much time to think about it because Lexie grabbed me by the arm and led me through the throng of people.

'Look over there!'

I gulped. There was no mistaking Donna Diamond, even in the faded light of the basement. She was exactly as she appeared in the tabloids, only much prettier and far more delicate looking. Her tiny frame was accentuated by her surgically enhanced breasts and her straightened long blonde hair completed the Barbie doll look. I'd expected to take an immediate dislike to her, but she looked so lovely, so utterly beguiling, that like the rest of the room, I couldn't take my eyes off her.

I took a sharp intake of breath.

'What is it?'

'Her tummy, look at her tummy.' The gentle swell of her belly lent her an air of vulnerability. She looked like an angel. A fallen angel. A pregnant angel.

Lexie made an unflattering snorting noise.

'Well, what did you expect? We knew she was pregnant, didn't we? That's the whole point of us being here. To persuade her to retract her story.'

I wasn't so sure now. Everything seemed clear-cut back at home. Donna was pregnant, Jimmy was certain it wasn't his, and it was simply a case of putting the record straight. Only now, seeing Donna in the flesh, I knew it wasn't that straightfor-ward. There was a growing baby involved. What if we'd got it wrong somehow? Could I really be cer-tain it wasn't Jimmy's baby? I only had his word for that and as much as I wanted to trust him, I was still racked with doubts.

'Come on,' said Lexie urgently, 'she's going to the loo. This is our chance!'

Reluctantly, I trundled after Lexie, a sense of dread filling my stomach.

'Ssh.' She turned and glared at me as we entered the cloakroom, holding a finger to her lips as my heels clicked across the floor. She crept along the linoleum on her tiptoes, secret squirrel style, expecting me to do the same. If it hadn't been so ridiculous, it might have been funny. 'She's in there,' she whispered, pointing to the one closed door.

Great! What were we supposed to do now? Conduct an interview in the small gap beneath the door? And all this hanging around was playing havoc with my bladder. I made for the next cubicle, but Lexie blocked my entrance.

'What do you think you're doing?' she hissed.

'I need a wee,' I hissed back.

'You can't!' Lexie mouthed. 'What if she comes out? No. I'm sorry. You're going to have to wait.'

I wasn't sure I could. I clamped my legs tightly together. All those orange juices and the cold air whipping around my nether regions was making me feel very uncomfortable, so I jiggled up and down on the spot, wishing Donna would hurry up.

Even so, it didn't stop us both jumping high in the air in surprise when the lock on the door clicked open and Donna breezed out, walking straight into our welcoming committee.

'Are you okay, girls?' she asked slowly, eyeing us suspiciously.

She was really tiny. Tiny frame, tiny features, big hair, big tits and a small, perfectly formed bump. It was a startling combination. I couldn't take my eyes off her.

'We wanted to have a word with you, Donna, if that's okay?' Lexie asked.

'Not really, I am out with my friends tonight, they'll be waiting for me,' she said, with only a hint of panic in her voice. She obviously thought we were over-enthusiastic fans. 'I can give you an autograph, if you'd like.'

'No,' said Lexie, her voice taking on a firmness I

didn't recognise. 'We don't want your autograph. We wanted to talk to you about something. Something personal, a delicate matter.'

'Really?' said Donna, suddenly wary. 'And what might that be, then?' She moved over to the washbasins and ran the cold water tap over her beautifully manicured nails. She turned around, giving us each in turn an appraising look.

'It's about the articles in the papers recently,' I ventured, 'about you and Jimmy. The baby.'

'Get lost!' she said with sudden spikiness. 'Who the hell do you think you are? My personal life is exactly that, personal.' Lexie and I shared a look. Hardly personal, when the whole sorry saga was being played out in the pages of the national rags. 'What's it to you, anyway?' asked Donna, her eyes flaring.

'We're friends of Jimmy,' said Lexie. 'Alice is a very close friend of his, actually, and we know Jimmy's not the father of your baby, Donna. You've made up lies about him and it's not fair. He's not here to defend himself, so we have to do it for him.'

'Huh. Don't be ridiculous. How do you know

what Jimmy got up to? Were you his guardian angel or something?' Donna's eyes ran up and down my body in barely concealed disgust.

'No, Alice is a medium,' added Lexie helpfully.

'Ha. A medium? Are you kidding me? I'd have her down as an extra-large any day.' She folded her arms with a sense of triumph.

I glared at Donna. Just because she was an under-nourished size zero who looked as though a slight gust of wind would have her wafting off down the High Street, it didn't give her the right to be downright rude to me. I pulled in my tummy as my gaze dropped to her small protruding bump and I bit back the nasty retort waiting to trip off my tongue.

'No, a spiritual medium. She can talk to dead people,' said Lexie in her most serious voice.

Donna's mouth gaped open, as she looked from Lexie to me.

'Jeez. You really are a couple of fruitcakes. I should have realised,' she said, sneering at my hastily put together outfit, making me feel even more exposed and self-conscious than I had all night, and I wouldn't have thought that was possible. She tossed the paper towels she'd been drying her hands on into the bin and walked towards the exit.

'We're deadly serious, Donna. Why did you do it? Making up all those lies about Jimmy, it's nasty and cruel.'

She stopped and turned around to face me.

'He's dead, love. Get over it. But I'll always have a part of him.' She cradled her bump in her hands. 'Now, I don't know what it is you're after, but you're wasting your time. And mine too. Now get out of my way, will you?'

'We don't want anything from you,' I called after her departing figure, blinking back the tears gathering in my eyes. I couldn't let Jimmy down. I'd promised him. This was my chance to put things right. 'We just want you to tell the truth. Do the right thing, Donna. For you and the baby. Think of your baby.'

Abruptly, she turned round to face me, her eyes locking on mine. As her dark eyes flared, I saw a flicker of vulnerability behind her stare, and in that moment I knew she was lying. I'd wanted to believe

Jimmy so much and now I knew for certain he'd been telling the truth after all.

'Fuck off,' she said with a quiet determination.

'Think about it, Donna. How will you feel having to live a lie for the rest of your life? Doesn't your baby have the right to know its true father?' My voice grew higher and higher with each word.

But she wasn't listening. She was halfway out the door. Scrabbling inside my handbag, I grabbed one of my business cards.

'Please, Donna. I'm begging you.' I ran after her, thrusting the card into her hands. 'Call me. We can talk about it. Please, give it some thought.'

'Come on,' said Lexie, putting an arm around my shoulder, 'you're wasting your breath.'

I slumped against the wall, adrenaline racing around my body.

'Should we go after her?'

'No, leave it. Give her time to think about it. She knows we're onto her. Now we just need to let her sweat for a few days.'

I hoped Lexie was right, but I had a feeling that Donna would be a much tougher nut to crack than we'd given her credit for.

'There is something I must do,' I said, suddenly remembering, and rushed into an empty cubicle. Sitting on the loo, I resolved, there and then, in my moment of joyous relief, that I would clear Jimmy's name, however long it might take and however difficult it might prove to be.

12

Defeated and downcast following our run-in with Donna, we drifted outside. The rain had stopped, but the temperature had dropped to sub-zero levels. There was no way I was going to be able to totter back down the main road in my state of undress.

'Shall we grab a taxi?' I asked Lexie.

'Good idea. Look, here's one now.'

She put one foot out in the road, one arm up in the air and a thumb and forefinger in her mouth, her whistle ricocheting off down the road. I smiled, grateful for having such a multi-talented sister. As the black cab pulled over a little way ahead, we broke into a run, eager to get out of the cold and into the warmth of the waiting car.

'Sorry, girls.' Two guys stepped out of the shadows just ahead of us, one of them placing a proprietary hand on the cab door. 'This one's ours.'

'I think not,' snapped Lexie, barging the larger of the two men out of the way. I winced, wishing Lexie would learn how to pick her fights. The guy must have been at least 6'2", was as broad as he was tall and had a 'I'm seriously disgruntled, don't mess with me' look upon his face.

'Alice?' The other guy's voice was incredulous, but unmistakably familiar. I swung round to see Damon standing there, noting the look of disbelief on his face as his eyes surveyed my exposed arms and legs. 'Good grief. It is you! What are you...?' He paused, shaking his head. 'Never mind. You'll catch your death dressed like that. Here,' he said, slipping off his jacket and handing it over, 'put this on.'

Damn, he was the last person I'd wanted to bump into, especially when he was looking so suave and sensibly dressed and I wasn't.

'Damon!' I said, tugging on my skirt to see if there was any way it would stretch to cover more of my bare legs, desperate to regain some decency. No such luck. I was about to reject his offer, but common sense got the better of me. 'Thanks so much,' I sighed, burying myself into the warmth of his wool coat, grateful that it swamped me a dozen times over.

'You know these people?' Lexie said with barely concealed disgust. She was still squaring up to Damon's friend, but had managed to manoeuvre herself into prime position for claiming the cab.

'Um, yes.' I laughed brightly, trying to defuse the tension. 'This is Damon. We used to work together at Merron.'

'Pleased to meet you,' said Damon, smiling, offering his hand to Lexie.

She attempted a smile, but failed, instead managing a friendly grimace.

'And this is Phil, a good friend of mine,' added Damon. 'I must apologise, he's not usually so competitive when it comes to hailing cabs, it's just that we've already lost out on a couple of taxis to other partygoers this evening. We were getting a bit desperate.'

I smiled inwardly. He didn't need to talk to me

about desperation. This evening, it could have been my middle name.

'Talking of which?' Phil was eyeing the cab warily, looking like a man who wasn't about to lose out on another ride.

'Well, we're going your way,' said Damon, 'shall we share this one? If that's okay?'

We all climbed into the back of the cab and thankfully, within minutes, Lexie and Phil had forgotten about their earlier contretemps and were chatting away like old friends.

'So, have you had a good evening?' asked Damon, as we settled down next to each other in our seats.

'Honestly? Dreadful. Really dreadful. We went to Planet 21.'

'I didn't have you down as a party animal, Alice.'

'I'm not! That's the point. It's been a long time since I've been to a nightclub, and after tonight, I hope it will be a long time before I have to go to another one.'

'That bad, eh? So why go then?'

'It's a long story. We were hoping to meet up

with someone, but things didn't turn out quite the way we planned.'

'Ah, I see.' He paused, looking at me through narrowed eyes. 'No, scrap that. I don't see at all. It all sounds very mysterious.'

We fell silent and my gaze drifted out of the cab window, transfixed by the hypnotic pull of the city's lights. I was grateful for Lexie and Phil's incessant chattering because I couldn't find anything to say to Damon. My mind was too full of the events of the evening – the memory of being locked in Jimmy's embrace was uppermost in my mind and then meeting Donna, seeing for myself the evidence of her pregnancy, had unsettled me more than I could have imagined.

If I'd had any doubts that Jimmy wasn't telling the truth about his relationship with Donna, then meeting her in the flesh had completely quashed that doubt. I could see in her eyes she was lying. And the look we'd shared told me she knew I had her sussed, but it didn't get over the fact that Donna was still very much pregnant, and everyone be-lieved that Jimmy Mack was the celebrity daddy.

'Yeah, it's going really well, thanks for asking.'

Damon's voice interrupted my musings. I turned to look at him, his face coming into startling focus as an awful dawning realisation hit me hard in the chest.

'Of course, the new venture! How's it going? It was a shame I missed your leaving do.' I scrunched up my shoulders, wishing I could disappear into the depths of his coat and not come out again. 'I'm so sorry. Things have been a bit manic for me these last few weeks.'

'Men problems,' Lexie piped up helpfully, before she returned her attentions to Phil.

'I meant to text you and tell you I wouldn't be able to make it, but it completely slipped my mind.' I felt dreadful, absolutely awful that I hadn't even bothered to send him a good luck text. What sort of person had I become? Since Jimmy's all-consuming presence had taken up residence in my life, there'd been little time for anything or anyone else.

'Hey, don't worry about it. I knew you'd come up with some lame excuse.' The twinkle in his eye told me he was joking, but still it made me feel like the most despicable person sitting in the cab. My cheeks tingled with shame. 'It's early days. There's a lot to do, starting up a new business,' he went on, 'but it's very exciting. I'm working much longer hours, if that's possible, but I'm really enjoying it. It's a challenge and I love a challenge.' He paused, a smile hovering on his lips as his gaze flittered across my face. 'Anyway, I'm glad I've bumped into you because there was something I wanted to ask you.'

'Okay,' I said curiously. Last time a man said that, it involved going to his own funeral and tracking down a pregnant celebrity glamour girl. What could I possibly have to fear from Damon?

'I need some help in putting in some systems for the new business. I hate admin, it's the bane of my life, but I reckoned if I got organised early on, even I might be able to keep track of the finances, etc. I wondered if you might be able to give me your expert opinion? A few tips. What do you reckon?'

'Of course. I'd be delighted to.' At least it would go a small way to making it up to Damon. And compared to all those other problems I had on my plate, a bit of admin would be child's play.

'Great. Perhaps we can meet for a coffee or something and talk through a few ideas. I'll give you a call in the next week or so and get something arranged, if that's okay with you?'

'Sure.'

'Hey, that's a great idea,' I heard Lexie saying, her voice barging into our conversation. I glanced over at her.

'What's that?' I asked, shifting in my seat.

'Phil suggested we go to the Irish Bar off the High Street for a nightcap. We'll be able to walk back to your place from there.'

'Actually, I'm really tired. Maybe we could...' I caught Lexie's practised death stare as my voice trailed away. My heart sank. The only place I wanted to go was home to tell Jimmy all the news and then into the depths of my big double bed.

'Hey, if you'd prefer not to, then don't worry about it,' added Damon.

'Really, Alice. I'm not going out with you again on a Saturday night. You're such a lightweight. It's only 12.30, the night's young.'

I gulped. The night felt positively ancient to me.

'Of course she'll come,' Lexie said, making up my mind for me.

The way she was fluttering her eyelashes at Phil,

I knew she'd never speak to me again if I backed out, and after everything she'd done for me this evening, I felt I didn't really have a choice.

Thankfully the bar was small, intimate and welcoming, with big squashy leather sofas and subdued lighting. A much nicer atmosphere to the cattle market feel inside Planet 21. They even managed to come up with the mug of steaming hot chocolate that I'd been hankering after all night.

'I can't tell you how much I need this!' I sighed, sipping the creamy frothy layer from the top of the mug.

Damon pointed discreetly to my lip, and I wiped away my foaming moustache with a smile.

It was after 2.30 a.m. by the time we got back to my flat. While Phil and Lexie were busy exchanging numbers outside the entrance to my block, Damon and I stood there, shuffling awkwardly from foot to foot in the cold.

'Right, well, I'll give you a call. Soon.'

'Sure,' I said, wishing Lexie would get a move on. Damon was a nice guy and good company too, but this evening had gone on far too long already. I needed to get home to Jimmy.

13

'Well,' said Lexie, filling up a tumbler with water from the tap, 'that wasn't such a wasted evening after all. What did you make of Phil?' She swooned exaggeratedly, flapping her hand in front of her face like an eighteenth-century heroine. 'I thought he was really cute.'

'Yes, he seemed very charming.' Well, he had from the little I'd had to do with him, because to be honest Lexie had monopolised his attention. 'Mind you, I suppose he was on his best behaviour, having escaped a decking from you.'

'Ha, that was a silly misunderstanding,' she giggled. 'And I did apologise. Lots of times!' She sat down on the sofa which would be doubling as her bed for the night, a dreamy look upon her face. 'What about you and Damon, though? You seemed to be getting on pretty well.'

'Yes, he's a nice guy,' I sighed, looking round, feeling strangely bereft that Jimmy hadn't bothered to wait up. I was certain he'd be in his usual place on the sofa, wanting to hear all the details of our meeting with Donna.

'Nice! Really, Alice, I worry about you at times. Damon is really hot and a great catch by the sound of things. You could do a lot worse, you know. You could have given the guy a bit of encouragement.'

'Don't be silly,' I laughed. 'Damon and I are just mates.' As if I had the time or the inclination for anything else at the moment. Jimmy was way too much of a distraction.

'Sorry, Lexie.' I stood up stretching my arms above my head. 'I have to go to bed. I'm so tired. Are you sure you'll be okay on the sofa?' Normally she'd stay in the spare room, but I couldn't turf Jimmy out when he'd taken it over as his own these last weeks. 'There are extra blankets in the airing cupboard if you need them.'

'Don't worry about me. I'll be fine. There's every possibility I'll be having very sweet dreams tonight,' she joked. 'Sleep well, darling.'

I tiptoed down the hall, mindful of not waking Jimmy, pausing to peer round the slightly ajar door of the guest room. Seeing his familiar outline beneath the covers was always reassuring, so discovering his bed was as pristine as it had been this morning, and more worryingly, still empty, I let out an involuntary cry.

'Alice? What is it? Are you okay?' Lexie was quickly beside me in the hallway.

'It's Jimmy. He's not here. I thought he'd gone to bed, but...'

'What, is that all?' She ran her hands through her hair, which tonight was a fetching lilac colour, looking every bit as fresh as I was feeling weary. 'He probably went on somewhere after you ran into him. Maybe he met up with some of his own type, you know,' she giggled, 'and they're all down at the local ghoulies and ghost rave.'

'It's not funny. Jimmy hasn't got anyone but me. Where would he go?' Admittedly, he had a habit of flitting in and out, making himself scarce when I had work or something else to see to, but he was always at home in the mornings and waiting for me again when I got in at night. It was our little routine. Besides, it was the middle of the night. What on earth could he be doing?

'Don't worry,' she said. 'He can't come to any harm. It's not as though anything terrible can happen to him because it already has. Ha ha! Think about it that way.'

I shot her a disapproving glance.

'You're not helping, Lexie. You're really not helping. What if he's gone?' I sank onto the bed, my head buzzing from the enormity of that thought. My heart thumped loudly inside my chest, the back of my neck feeling hot and sweaty. 'What if they came to get him while we were out?'

'You're not making any sense, Alice. What if who came for him?'

'The people up there. The heavenly authorities. Angels. I don't know what you call them, but whoever it is who's going to take him across to the other side. Perhaps now we've made contact with Donna and she knows we know the truth about what happened, Jimmy's spirit has been released.

That's it! I didn't even get the chance to say goodbye.'

I sank down onto Jimmy's vacant bed, tears rushing to my eyes.

'Well,' she said, sitting down next to me and putting an arm around my shoulder, 'that's a good thing, isn't it? Saves you a job.'

'Lexie!'

'No, I don't mean it in a bad way, but you knew he had to go sometime, and you were wondering how it would happen. Perhaps, this way, it's the problem sorted for you.'

'I really hope not,' I cried, sobbing. 'I don't want him to go. Not yet. There were things I needed to say.' How would I ever manage without Jimmy? In such a short space of time, he'd come to fill a huge hole in my life.

'Stop it now.' Lexie handed me a tissue from the box on the side. 'We don't know that he has gone, do we? I still reckon he's gone out partying. Probably found some hot little ghostly chick to make out with. You mark my words, he'll be back any minute now, up to his normal antics. Freaking the friggin' life out of me.'

I forced a smile. The flat, his room, felt strangely empty without his all-pervasive presence.

'You're tired and emotional. It's been a taxing evening. Get to sleep and when you wake up, I'm sure he'll be back.'

'Do you really think so?'

'I know so,' said Lexie, kissing me on the forehead. 'Now get to sleep.'

Exhausted, I took Lexie at her word and fell asleep there and then, without any thought as to what Jimmy would do if and when he got home and wanted his bed back. When I did finally wake up, I thought I must have only been asleep for a matter of minutes, but the alarm clock on the bedside table confirmed it was past ten the next morning. I shot out of bed with a start.

'Jimmy?' I yawned, padding through to the living room. He had to be home by now, sitting on the sofa, sipping tea from a mug, looking apologetic.

'Morning,' said Lexie, lazily opening one eye, shuffling herself up one end of the sofa to make room for me. Admittedly, she was wrapped in the duvet, but I was pretty certain she wasn't hiding Jimmy under there too.

'Oh, no,' I sighed, 'is Jimmy not back?'

'If he's got any sense, he'll still be tucked up in a bed somewhere.' She sat up, stretching out her little legs, reminding me of a good-natured pixie. 'Jeez, it's early. Fancy a brew?'

'But, Lexie, where the hell is he?'

'Well, hopefully not there!'

I glared at her, biting on my lip to stop the tears escaping from my eyes.

'Nah, don't worry,' she went on, 'he definitely had a few brownie points under his belt. Him being a much-loved entertainer and all that. He'll be on his way up the upwards escalator, rest assured.'

I sighed, sniffing morosely.

'I didn't think he'd be taken so quickly after seeing Donna. I thought we'd have a couple of days' grace. He can't just go like this without saying good-bye. It's not right.'

She dropped her head to the side, pulling a sad face. 'Let me get you that cup of tea. You look as though you need one.'

I rested my head in my hands and wept quietly.

Lexie was right. I knew Jimmy would have to leave at some point, but I wasn't ready for it like this, so suddenly. Pain clenched a tight knot in my stomach.

'Tea,' offered Lexie, a few moments later, handing me a mug. 'Just look at you,' she said, noticing my reddened puffy eyes. 'If you're that worried, why don't you try giving him a call?'

Gawd, she was testing my patience.

'Top of the range mobile phones aren't standard issue for newly recruited ghosts, you know.'

'No, but you can summon him, can't you? By the power of thought. Or something.' She waved her hands in the air with a flourish. Who did she think I was all of a sudden? Samantha from *Bewitched*? 'I thought you had this special thing going on?'

'I think it's a one-way arrangement,' I sighed. 'It's Jimmy who can do the magic stuff, not me.'

'Shame,' Lexie sighed, sounding wholly uninterested as she dunked a Rich Tea biscuit in her tea and delved into the weekend papers.

If Jimmy had gone for good, how would my life ever be the same again?

There would be no one waiting for me when I came home at night.

No one to laugh with over re-runs of *Friends*.

No one to make a cup of tea for me in the mornings or to put a delicious meal on the table of an evening.

No one to care for me.

And I would miss Jimmy for simply being Jimmy. His huge wide smile, those deep grey inquisitive eyes, his warm nut-brown laugh that echoed out over the flat.

It was almost too awful to contemplate.

Instead, I stared into my empty mug, trying not to think about it, the silence and emptiness of the flat oppressive.

'Jimmy!' I screamed, inwardly. Why was he doing this to me?

Moments later, a cool rush of air swept around the flat as his familiar dulcet tones sounded in my ear.

'Blimey, why all the long faces? Has someone died?'

'Jimmy!' I leapt up off the sofa. 'For goodness'

sake! Where on earth have you been? I've been worried sick.'

'Thank the Lord for that,' said Lexie resignedly, as she picked up her clothes and wandered towards the bathroom. 'The spooky wanderer returns, does he? Do us a favour, Jimmy, next time you want to go walkabout, could you let the boss know? She's been in a dreadful state all night.'

'Ah, tea!' Jimmy, seemingly oblivious to my distress, spotted our empty mugs sitting on the table. 'I'll just grab myself one, if you don't mind, it's been a long night.'

How dare he, was my first thought, as I grabbed him by the lapels. His warm familiar masculine scent reassured me and angered me at the same time. Who did he think he was, waltzing in like a paying guest without any regard to my feelings?

'Where the bloody hell have you been?' All the worry that had been festering inside over the last few hours erupted in a frenzy of pummelling on Jimmy's chest. 'Why didn't you tell me you wouldn't be coming home?'

Bemused, his eyes scanned my face, before looking down and noticing my attempts to do his ghostly form some serious damage. Clearly, I was having no impact whatsoever.

'Hey, hey, hey.' He gently removed my hands from his chest, holding my wrists down by my sides. 'I went to catch up with a few people, that was all.' He wiped the tears from my cheeks with the backs of his thumbs, pushing the hair out of my eyes. 'It was a last-minute thing. When you got back last night, I saw you with that guy,' he waved a hand in the air, 'um, the flash one with...'

'You mean Damon?'

'Yep, that's him. I reckoned you wouldn't want me around cramping your style, so I decided to make myself scarce.'

'Aw, Jimmy, you didn't need to do that. We went for a drink, that's all. We bumped into them when we came out of the club. Damon and I used to work together, and Lexie got chatting to his friend Phil.' I could hear myself gabbling, explaining, apologising. For what, though, I didn't quite understand. But then it came to me. I didn't want Jimmy thinking Damon was anything other than a friend.

'That's not a hint of jealousy I detect from the

ghostly quarter, is it?' Lexie's voice wafted from down the hallway.

'Don't be silly,' I said, jumping to Jimmy's defence as I rolled my eyes at my sister's silly comment. Pure unadulterated relief filtered through my veins at being with him again. 'Don't worry, she'll be going home soon. You should have told me, though, Jimmy. I was worried. I thought you'd gone for good, that I'd never see you again.'

'Sorry.' He glanced at the floor, looking contrite, and then turned his gaze on my face. 'You're right, I should have told you. It was rude of me, disappearing like that. I suppose it's only natural you're going to have your own life to lead.' And if I hadn't known better, I might have been inclined to agree with Lexie's earlier assertion.

Now the tears ran freely down my face, my shoulders juddering with relief. He delved in his pockets and pulled out a hankie, and made a half-hearted attempt at mopping me up before giving it up as a bad job and handing the crisp white cloth over to me. I nodded my thanks and blew my nose noisily, which seemed to make him laugh. I sniffed, feeling ridiculously happy and desperately despondent at the same time.

Jimmy had come home this time, but he could quite easily have disappeared, literally without a trace. And where would that have left me? I'd invested so much time and energy into helping him find his rightful place in the universe that I should have been overjoyed at the thought of him moving on. Only now, looking up into those deep grey eyes, his charcoal hair falling over his face, I felt an overwhelming sense of sadness that I'd be losing him very soon.

Imperceptibly, he'd made himself irreplaceable in my life, and I didn't know how I'd ever manage without him.

He took my hands in his, holding me at arm's length, looking imploringly into my eyes.

'Let's make a pact, Alice. When I do finally have to go,' he said, as if reading my mind, 'I promise that I'll come and say a proper goodbye before I leave. How about that?'

My stomach churned under the intensity of his gaze.

'That sounds good.' Our hands interlocked, he

squeezed my fingers. I'd have been content to stay like that, gazing up into his eyes the entire day, but the shuffling noises behind me distracted my attention.

'Well, I'll leave you to it, then. Now that normal service has been resumed.' Lexie appeared from the bathroom, clutching her overnight bag in her hands, looking tired and uncharacteristically vulnerable without any make-up on.

'Darling, Lexie!' I ran over to her, throwing my arms around her neck. The events of the last twenty-four hours, twenty-four days or however long it had been since Jimmy had bulldozed into my life had left me feeling strangely wobbly and tearful. My sister, my dear lovable and infuriating sister. What would I have done without her?

'Thanks so much for everything, you know, last night and all that. For being so understanding. I couldn't have done it without you.'

'Hey, anytime, you know that,' she said. 'I'm only sorry we didn't get a better result from Donna Diamond. Still, we'll catch up with her yet. Don't you worry about it.'

'Thanks, darling,' I said, giving her a big kiss.

With Lexie and Jimmy on my team, everything would be all right, I felt certain.

'Yeah, thanks, Lexie,' said Jimmy, wafting past her and whispering in her ear. 'I'll see you soon.'

'Ugh... that pesky ghost!' she yelped, flapping her hand around the back of her neck and leaping up and down on the spot. 'Would you not do that? Tell him, Alice. It's seriously freaky.'

'Behave yourself,' I laughed, nudging him in the ribs with my elbow, as we watched Lexie dance down the hallway.

After breakfast, we decided to head for the great outdoors. The atmosphere in the flat was becoming oppressive and besides, the sun had been filtering through the picture windows, beckoning us outside, the forecast for the rest of the day bright sunshine.

Brickhill Country Park was only ten minutes away and a haven for wildlife, dog-walkers, young families and courting couples.

Walking hand in hand with Jimmy along the pathway that led to the boating lake, I had to keep reminding myself that outside of our little fragilely constructed bubble, none of this was real. To the

man pushing his young son along on his toy motor-
bike, I was a single woman taking a Sunday
morning stroll alone. To the teenage couple gently
teasing each other, I was probably a figure of pity
and ridicule. To the guy loitering behind the dust-
bins, I was fair game.

'All right, love?' he asked, a sneer moulding his
face.

'She's out of your league, mate,' called Jimmy,
putting a protective arm around my shoulder as we
sauntered past. I laughed, confusing the guy with my
reaction as he shook his head dismissively. If I'd
been alone, I'd have felt vulnerable and frightened
and would probably have turned back onto the main
path, but with Jimmy beside me I'd felt protected, a
feeling I relished, and something I realised had been
sorely missing from my life. Someone to lean on.

Maybe, in the absence of a real live man in my
life, I needed something else. A dog, perhaps, I
thought, smiling as a scruffy-haired mutt scam-
pered past. Whatever it was, the hole that I hadn't
even known existed in my life had been given a
temporary fix by Jimmy's special brand of spiritual

healing. The trouble was, I knew it was only a for-the-moment arrangement.

'To be honest, Jimmy, it was all a bit of a disaster last night. We did our best, but we had to pounce on Donna in the loos. It wasn't the most conducive atmosphere to getting her on our side. And when she heard what we had to say, it only made matters much worse.'

'I bet.'

'She's very pretty, isn't she? Much prettier than she seems on telly and in the mags. Up close, you can definitely see the natural beauty beneath all the glitz.' It wouldn't have surprised me if Jimmy had slept with her, after all. Any red-blooded male would have their head turned by someone as desirable as Donna.

Jimmy scrunched up his nose, as though he'd just caught a whiff of something unsavoury.

'You think? She's not my type, that's for sure.'

'Really? And what's your type then, Jimmy?' The outdoors air made me bold.

He stopped and spun me round to face him.

'Someone like you,' he said looking at me intently. 'Yeah, I suppose you'd do, with your funny ideas and quirky ways.'

'Thanks a bunch,' I said, laughing away the compliment, but my body couldn't ignore the implication. My stomach scrambled and I felt the back of my throat tighten.

'She was very cool and collected,' I said, linking my arm through his. 'She wasn't about to admit she'd made the whole thing up, but I could tell by her eyes she was lying.'

'You weren't prepared to take my word for that, then?'

'Yes, but...' I blushed, knowing he had me sussed. I'd wanted to believe him more than anything, but it was difficult when all the national papers were telling a very different story.

'Hey, don't worry about it. I'd have been the same,' he admitted. 'The trouble is, the rest of the population will be thinking the same as you.' He paused to pick up a stone, and flicked it with his wrist into the water. It skimmed along the surface, and we watched the ripples spreading outwards. 'It's not the way I want to be remembered, though.'

'I know,' I said. I hated seeing him so hurt and

downcast. As if being dead wasn't enough, he had all this other rubbish to contend with too. 'We'll go and see Donna again. Perhaps now she's had a chance to think about it, she'll realise what she's done, how wrong it is, and change her mind and tell the truth.'

'You reckon? I doubt it somehow,' he said, his brow furrowing. 'There'd be more chance of me coming back from the dead!'

'Stop it!' I hated him talking like that, reminding me that he didn't belong here.

'You know,' he said, then paused, bending down to pick up another pebble, throwing it with more venom this time. It plopped with a thud deep into the water. 'I went to see my parents last night.'

'Did you?' My heart twisted. So that's where he'd been.

'Yeah. Mum's in a bad way. This whole baby thing has really shaken her up. She was just coming to terms with the fact that I'm not around any more and now this. She's horrified. She doesn't want to believe it, and yet... she doesn't know what to believe.'

His voice trailed away as we wandered down to

the water's edge and watched as a mother duck and her ducklings followed behind two small girls trailing bread into the water.

'What can I do? It's so frustrating. She thinks her first grandchild will be coming into the world and she's wondering what part she'll play in that child's life. I need her to know the truth, to tell her not to worry, but I can't.' He sighed, a ghostly sigh, heavy with regret. 'You know, I had a good go at telling her, but obviously she wasn't hearing me. I even thought about trying out one of my few ghostly tricks, but decided against it. I didn't want her to worry any more than she is already.'

'No, keep the tricks purely for Lexie's benefit, hey?' I smiled, wishing though, for once, it could be his mum who could see and hear him, not me.

'The thing is, she could spend a lot of time and emotional energy in getting to see and bonding with a baby that isn't even mine.'

It was a terrible thought. That Jimmy, a dead man, had to live with the lie was one thing, but to think that the repercussions would filter through to his family and friends, affecting their whole lives too. Whatever my personal feelings about Donna, I was sure she couldn't be aware of the devastation she was causing by the fact of one little lie. No one could be that callous.

'I could go and see your mum, tell her the true situation.' Desperation coloured my words. If only there was something I could do to help.

'Hmm, but then it's just your word against Donna's. It might just make matters worse for Mum.'

'I suppose,' I said. 'There's always a DNA test, if it comes to it. I know it's not something you'd want to insist on, but if it's going to prove things once and for all, then it might be the only answer.'

Jimmy nodded.

'Do you know, this whole thing has been a nightmare?' He reached out a hand to my shoulder, the intensity of his gaze on my face holding me captive. 'But the one thing that's made it bearable is having you here at my side. You've been so supportive. I mean it, Alice, I don't know what I would have done without you.'

He placed a feather-light kiss on my forehead, tipping my head back with his finger on my chin. As my eyes closed involuntarily, I felt an overwhelming surge of happiness, tempered with a stab of loss and regret. If I'd been fighting my feelings for weeks, I knew now with a thud that I couldn't hang onto them for a moment longer. They'd been swept away by a ghost.

'I just wish there was more I could do to help,' I said, looking up into his grey soulful eyes, realising I was lost there.

'Just you being here helps, Alice. I can't tell you how much.' He dropped his gaze for a moment before looking up at me with a huge grin on his face. 'God, I am so hungry!' He rubbed his tummy, bringing me back to the moment. 'How about you?'

'Ravenous,' I agreed. It must have been all the fresh air playing havoc with my appetite and my emotions.

'There's a café next to the car park. Come on,' he laughed, taking off. 'I'll race you.'

'Jimmy! Wait. I'm not running, don't be silly!' But he wasn't listening, he'd disappeared off into the distance and I could only limp after him, laughing at his exuberance and enthusiasm.

When I caught up with him a few minutes later, he was already at the buffet, eyeing up the selection.

'What kept you?' he asked, grinning, pointing me in the direction of the plastic trays.

I was panting, but I seemed to be in a constant state of breathless anticipation these days, so that was nothing new. 'I was going to let you have a piece of my bacon,' I said churlishly, 'but I'm not so sure now.'

'Well, to be on the safe side, we ought to get enough for both of us,' he said, loading my plate high, first with bacon, then with sausages, tomatoes, mushrooms, fried bread, two eggs and, finally, black pudding.

'Yuk,' I said eyeing it warily.

'What? It's delicious. You don't know what you're missing out on. Now, don't forget the toast,' he said, putting the entire contents of the bread basket on my plate.

At the till, the young sylph-like cashier surveyed my tray with undisguised disgust.

'Someone's hungry,' she said, raising a perfectly arched eyebrow.

'Yep, I'm in training,' I said airily, 'for the London Marathon.' I did a little jog on the spot for demonstration purposes. 'I need plenty of proteins and carbs. I'll have all this run off by lunchtime.'

Her mouth fell open and I noticed the small shake of her head.

'Come on, my very favourite, highly toned athlete.' Jimmy gave me an affectionate slap on the backside, making me squirm and giggle on the spot. 'I'll race you.'

'Must dash,' I called to the cashier who was giving me a very dismissive look as I jogged off, following my favourite ghost to the table.

15

The week in the run-up to the Charity Ball was absolutely manic at work, so I was relieved when Jimmy explained he had plans of his own.

'Listen, Alice,' he said, grabbing my hand one morning as I was about to leave for work, 'I've got some stuff to catch up with this week, so don't worry if you don't see me for a few days.'

'Oh?'

'Yeah, seeing my parents the other day made me realise I have some unfinished business to sort out. I want to pop in on a few people, say my goodbyes. So no freaking out if I'm AWOL for a while. I promise I'll be fine and I'll be back as soon as I can.'

'What's happened, Jimmy? Have you heard something, then? You'd tell me if you'd been given a leaving date, wouldn't you?'

Jimmy shook his head, laughing.

'I might be wrong, but I don't think I'll be receiving written notification through the post. But hey, if I do, you'll be the first to know.'

'Okay,' I said, feeling foolish. Ever since we'd met up with Donna, I'd been in a heightened sense of panic, thinking Jimmy would be taken at any moment. Despite his reassurances to the contrary, how would I know if he'd ever come back again? And would he even have any say in the matter?

A shiver rippled down my spine at the thought of him wandering off on his own again and those poor unsuspecting people on the end of an unexpected visit from the ghostly apparition of Jimmy Mack. He'd probably scare them half to death. Mind you, he was looking particularly delectable this morning. In what was becoming his daily uniform of dark jeans and fitted white T-shirt, the strong hard lines of his body were accentuated. And I don't know whether it was my imagination, but it seemed with each passing day that Jimmy's eyes grew a shade darker, their depths becoming more intense and soul-bearing. I was sure the flecks of silver in his hair were becoming more plentiful too, and the pallor of his skin gave an ethereal effect, sending my stomach into freefall.

'Okay, just be careful out there.' Who knew what dangers were lurking in the murky places he was frequenting? 'Do you think there's a whole host of people out there making from-beyond-the-grave visits? It's a bit creepy, when you think about it.'

'Thanks. People like me, you mean?' asked Jimmy, looking offended. 'I don't know. I've a feeling there's not that many of us around. Would be nice to meet a fellow in-betweener, but I think I could be something of an anomaly.'

He gave half a smile and my heart twisted in sympathy.

Not for the first time, I was reminded what a precarious predicament he was in. Stuck between one world and another. And for how long we just didn't know. Never being able to find any real peace or contentment. Forever caught betwixt and between.

'Well, you're a very lovely anomaly,' I said,

stroking away a thread from his T-shirt. I'd miss him; his easy companionship, the sight of his coffee mug around the place, the scent of his skin. 'Just be careful, won't you?' I reminded him again.

'I'll be fine,' he said, leaning in to kiss me on the cheek, his touch sending tingles down the length of my body, leaving me wanting so much more. 'I'll catch up with you later in the week.'

By Friday night, after a hectic few days at work, I was hot with anticipation at the thought of seeing him again. After walking through the door to my flat, I kicked off my shoes, deposited my jacket on the back of a chair, my jumper on the coffee table and my jewellery on the small bureau.

I ran the bath, lit my two Jo Malone orange blossom candles and put on some mellow Al Green in the background before helping myself to a large glass of chilled Sauvignon Blanc. Taking my wine with me, I eased myself into the bath, immediately feeling the tensions of the week melt away. I was still there an hour later, when the water had turned an uncomfortable lukewarm and my skin had taken on the fetching crumpled appearance of a Chinese fighting dog, and I was just stepping out and easing myself into my big fluffy dressing gown when the familiar cool whoosh of air that always heralded Jimmy's arrival whipped beneath the bathroom door.

'Hi, honey, I'm home!'

'Hey!' The deep warm tones of his voice immediately lifted my spirits. Relief flooded through my bones, knowing he was home at last.

'Hang on, I'll be there in a moment.' Hurriedly, I rubbed my hair dry with a towel, glancing cursorily at my reflection in the mirror. Devoid of make-up, my skin was glowing pink and my eyes had taken on a piggy quality. Probably not the best look for welcoming home a gorgeous man on a Friday night, but knowing what a gentleman Jimmy was, he would probably pretend not even to notice.

'Hi, how are you? How was your week?' I said, from beneath the hood of my dressing gown, as I emerged in a fuggy glow from the bathroom door.

'I hope I didn't interrupt your bath, did I?' Gently he pushed down my hood and placed a kiss on my cheek as if it was the most natural thing in the world to do. I had to restrain myself from standing on tiptoes, flinging my arms around his neck and smothering him with tiny little kisses.

'No, I was finished, anyway.' Banishing such inappropriate thoughts, I contented myself instead with a gentle pat of his back, wondering again what the social etiquette was for greeting very good-looking ghosts.

'Good. Let me get you a nice glass of wine.' He wandered off in the direction of the kitchen. 'What do you fancy for supper, a takeaway or shall I make us an omelette?'

'An omelette sounds delicious, but you don't want to be cooking.' For some reason, I felt ridiculously self-conscious, as though I was meeting Jimmy all over again for the first time. 'You've only just got in. I'm sure there's a pizza in the freezer we can bung in the oven.'

'Nonsense,' he said, his face beaming from around the kitchen door, 'it won't take me a minute. I got you a present, by the way. Take a look in the bag there.'

A very expensive-looking carrier bag stood proudly on the floor.

'What is it?'

'Well, it won't be a surprise if I tell you, will it? Have a look,' he laughed.

Curiously, I picked up the white glossy bag with the fancy gold lettering. Peering inside, I pulled out a cloud of pink tissue before my fingers landed on the rich, silky material.

'Jimmy, it's beautiful,' I cried, lifting out the dress and holding it aloft, my hands running over the expensive fabric.

'Well, I thought you couldn't go to the ball without a knock-them-dead dress to wow them in.'

'Oh, Jimmy!'

That was typical of him. So thoughtful. I'd mentioned how I'd probably end up wearing my old faithful little black dress, not having the time or the money or the inclination to go out and find something new, and now he'd gone and done the job for me. And what a fabulous dress it was. The colour of deep blush wine, it had a plunging neckline with a gentle ruffle leading from the décolletage down through the centre of the floaty fabric. It would skim the body in all the right places and was guaranteed to look stunning.

On the right person.

Only I wasn't the right person, I thought, sighing wistfully.

From years of bitter experience, I knew that finding a dress to fit my decidedly non-standard figure wasn't nearly as simple as Jimmy might have imagined. There was always some part of my body, my big boobs, my long body or the too-wide hips, that took exception to any outfit I tried on, which was why, invariably, I ended up going home empty-handed from any shopping blitz. Never in a million years would this beautiful dress ever fit me.

'Where did you get it from, though? You're not going to try and tell me this has come from the supermarket, too?'

'No, don't be silly, Alice. I ran it up on the sewing machine.'

'Oh yeah, right! Now who's being silly? Come on, tell me! I can't possibly accept anything that's come from some dodgy underworld dealing. I don't mind keeping company with a ghost, but I don't want to be arrested as an accessory for handling stolen goods.'

Jimmy raised his eyebrows and shook his head.

'You have an overactive imagination, do you

know that? I'm sorry to disappoint you, but I'm not involved in any dodgy dealings. I've told you, I made the dress. If you don't want it, you only have to say so.'

'You made it? No way! How did you do that?'

'Well, first I pinned the pattern on the material and then...'

'No! Not how did you make it, just how did you manage to do that? I don't understand.'

'When I went to my mum's. It's been a few years since I've used a sewing machine, but after a few false starts, it all came back to me. My mum's a dressmaker by trade. I learnt to sew when I was very young.'

'Are you serious? That is so cool.'

'Not when I was a kid, it wasn't!' His warm laugh caressed me. 'I quickly gave up sewing when I started getting grief from the lads at school, but it's one of those things that stays with you. I wanted you to have something special for the ball and this was the only way I knew how.'

'You did that for me?' My heart swelled. 'Where did you get the material from? And the pattern?'

'The material was from Mum's attic, she has a

whole stash up there, and the pattern... well, don't you recognise the design? You said how much you liked the dress. That's why I chose it.' He picked up the glossy magazine on the coffee table and opened it to the centre double-page spread showing celebrities at a recent awards ceremony.

'Flipping heck, it's the same dress! And you made it? I can't believe it. That is so amazing, Jimmy. Thank you so much.'

'My pleasure. Aren't you going to try it on, then?'

And now I'd have to let Jimmy down. After all the trouble he'd been to as well.

'I will do, later,' I said, carefully placing the dress back in its tissue.

'No. Go and pop it on now. I insist. While I'm doing the tea. I'm dying to see what it will look like on. When I saw that colour, I just knew, instinctively, that it would suit you.'

I smiled, weakly. He wasn't going to take no for an answer. At least Jimmy would see with his own eyes the futility of the situation.

'Won't be a minute, then,' I said, wandering back

into the bedroom. Trying on clothes was a nightmare at the best of times, but with a willing and enthusiastic audience waiting, it only made matters
much worse. I slipped off my robe and stepped into
the dress. Surprisingly, it didn't get stuck over my
hips or around my tummy and zipped up easily at
the back. It felt gloriously feminine and delicate
against my skin, the soft folds of fabric swishing
around my body, my bare nipples reacting to its silky
touch. I spun round to examine my reflection in the
mirror and gasped. I stepped forward, peering into
the glass, my hand instinctively reaching out to the
unfamiliar image, checking it was really me. Amazing. The dress fitted perfectly. The fluted sleeves sat
perfectly on my shoulders and the red silk fabric
swept over my body, accentuating my breasts and
waist and hips. It could have been tailor-made.

'Are you all right in there?' Jimmy called from
the kitchen.

'Yes,' I said, suddenly feeling shy. 'I'm just
coming.'

Slowly I eased open the door and walked towards Jimmy in the living room.

'What do you think, then?' I asked, giving him a self-conscious twirl.

'Whoa!' Jimmy, his eyes wide, dropped the tea towel he was holding to the floor. 'You look fan-bloody-tastic. Amazing!' He let out a long slow whistle, shaking his head. 'I knew the dress would suit you, but I couldn't have imagined this... wow is all I can say!'

I laughed, embarrassed. I had no make-up on, and my hair was still damp, clinging to the sides of my face unflatteringly.

'But how did you get the sizing right? I can never find anything to fit me and this, I don't believe it, but it fits like a glove. It could have been made for me.'

'It was made for you, Alice. By me. Your measurements, I have them all up here, imprinted on my brain.' He tapped the side of his head, smiling, and the thought of him knowing my body so intimately made my insides melt with desire.

'That's so cool. I really do have my very own Tailor of Gloucester living with me.'

I threw my arms around his neck and kissed

him on the cheek, his musky masculine scent reaching my nostrils.

Jimmy threw back his head and laughed.

'I'm just glad you like it,' he went on. 'Cinderella will go to the ball after all! Now go, take it off!' A seductive smile rested on his lips, but his masterful tone and the dark dangerous look in his eye sent a swirl of heightened anticipation coursing through my body.

A few nights ago, when I went to that club with Lexie, I was definitely the ugly sister, but in this wonderful dress made by Jimmy, basking in the glow of his adoration, I could definitely imagine myself as Cinderella. The only trouble was, I was certain my very own Prince Charming would be doing a bunk sometime soon.

16

'Look at you!' Tara from Accounts made a beeline for me across the busy foyer, lifting my arms up wide and looking me up and down. 'Don't you scrub up well?'

'Thanks,' I said, blushing. I suppose the transformation was a bit extreme. From sober-suited PA to glitzy reluctant sex-kitten, even I was surprised by the result. 'I thought I'd better make the effort.'

'Well, you've certainly done that. I love your dress. It's fabulous. Tell me, where did you get it from?'

I smiled smugly, thinking of Jimmy's proud face when he'd handed over the gown. What could I say? That my very own live-in ghost had made it for me? I'm sure Tara thought me a bit stand-offish as it was. I didn't want her thinking I was completely doolally as well.

'I found it in a little boutique in... in the country.'

'Really? Whereabouts?'

'Um... close to where my aunt lives. A small village. In the middle of nowhere. I'm sure you've never heard of it.'

She raised a doubtful eyebrow at me.

'Nanchester... dale,' I said, with as much conviction as I could muster. I just hoped to goodness she didn't know such a place.

'Hmmm, you're right, I've never heard of it. You'll have to give me the details sometime. I'm always on the lookout for exciting new designers.'

'Sorry to interrupt, Alice...' Just at the right moment, Simon appeared at my side, accompanied by a very familiar face. 'Can I introduce you to Barney Roberts?'

I'd never been so pleased to see anyone before in my life. Hopefully neither of them would give a flying fig about where I did my shopping.

'Hello, Barney. It's lovely to meet you. Thanks so much for stepping in at such short notice. We're really delighted to have you here.'

'My pleasure.' Barney smiled, his gaze landing on my cleavage and almost taking up residence there. 'But with such a generous fee offered, you made it very difficult for me to refuse,' he laughed.

Jimmy had waived the five-figure sum, donating it instead to the company's charity, but obviously Barney had no such qualms about accepting the fee.

'And I get to sit next to the most beautiful woman in the room,' he said, taking me by the arm. 'This gig just gets better and better.'

We sat down at our table, with me sandwiched between Barney and Simon. On the other side of Barney was the head of Human Resources, Janine Malin, but after a cursory hello, Barney pointedly turned his back on her and focused all his attention on me. I edged my chair away from him as discreetly as I could.

Funny to think that had it not been for Jimmy's tragic accident, I would have been meeting him for the first time tonight instead of Barney. The thought was surreal. I'd got to know Jimmy as a ghostly presence, coming to love his easy charm and self-deprecating humour, but as I was his only ally in the strange world he inhabited, our relation-ship had been unnaturally intense, intimate even. Without us being thrown together in such unusual circumstances, would our relationship ever have got beyond first base? Would I have liked Jimmy or been irritated by him, like I was being irritated by Barney now?

He'd edged his chair back closer to mine and was giving me a blow-by-blow account of his career history, the people he knew and generally just how marvellous he was. In the flesh, Barney Roberts was much smaller, scrawnier and infinitely less likeable than he appeared on screen. Jimmy had been right. His proximity made my skin crawl. I couldn't imagine what it was I ever saw in him.

'What people don't realise is that I was being lined up to take over Jimmy Mack's daytime show, even before he died.'

'Really?' Hearing Jimmy's name bandied about so casually brought me up with a start.

'Yeah, Jimmy was definitely on his way out as

one of the major players on TV. He'd had his moment. Quite honestly, I can't understand all the fuss there's been about his death. I mean, he was clearly past his best. Maybe it was a blessing in disguise that he went when he did. While he was still at the top of the game.'

My mouth gaped open, but words failed to materialise. He'd only been dead for a matter of a few weeks. Didn't the man have any respect at all?

'Jimmy would never have fallen out of favour with the general public,' I said, with a conviction I didn't know I possessed. 'The people loved him. He was a real superstar and a perfect gentleman too.'

'Everything okay?' Simon leant across, smiling.

'Absolutely fine.' Barney smiled. 'Although I think your beautiful secretary here might have preferred the company of your first choice tonight, Mr Jimmy Mack. She was something of a fan, I think.' He laughed, showing off a full set of dazzling veneers.

Simon raised his eyebrows at me, smiling questioningly.

'We were just saying what a shame it was about Jimmy. Such a lovely man.' My gaze drifted around the room. Would I survive another couple of hours being stuck with this idiot, especially when he seemed unable to look me in the eye? I pulled my dress up at the front, clasping my hands together over my chest.

'Yes, terrible. Do they know yet what caused the accident?' Simon asked.

'No, it's all a bit of a mystery. Mind you, between you, me and the gatepost, I have a feeling that there was a lot of stuff we didn't know about Jimmy Mack. I mean who'd have thought he was shagging Donna Diamond. The old rogue!'

'You don't believe everything you read in the newspapers, do you?' I snapped. 'Excuse me for a moment, would you, please?' I slid my chair backwards, eager to get away before I did or said something I knew I would regret, leaving Simon and Barney to their conversation.

In the loos, I was glad for a moment's respite and was surprised to see from my reflection that I was looking uncharacteristically cool and polished and altogether like someone else much more sophisticated than me, despite my insides feeling like a quivering mess. What a slimeball Barney was, I thought as I wiped away a smudge of mascara from beneath my eye. Everything he said seemed to be a slight against Jimmy and he didn't show one ounce of compassion towards his ex-colleague. The man was so up himself, so full of his own self-importance, it was untrue. If it hadn't been a work function, then I would have definitely told him where to go by now.

Deep breaths, I told myself, as I smoothed my hands down over my dress. I stopped for a moment and marvelled at the image of the girl looking back at me. The dress was stunning, there was no doubting that, but I recognised something else in my reflection, a glowing confidence and self-assurance that I was certain hadn't been there a few weeks ago. Even when Jimmy wasn't around, I felt protected by his warmth, enthusiasm and love. Putting up with a slimeball like Barney would be a doddle. Taking one last glance over my shoulder, I left to face the next round. Only a few more hours to go, then I'd be back at home, regaling Jimmy with all the gory details.

'Well, hello, sweetheart, I wondered where you'd got to.'

'Barney!' My voice rang out cheerfully, but a cold dread spread through my bones. He must have been lying in wait.

'I'm sure that boss of yours is a great guy, but boy, he's so dreary. All that corporate bollocks is very dull. I don't know how you put up with it, day in and day out.' He laughed, slipping his hand around my waist. 'I followed your lead and made my excuses and left.'

'I only came out to get a breath of fresh air. We ought to get back.' I firmly removed his hand. 'We don't want to miss the main course, do we?'

'Mmm, I don't know,' he said, leaning forward and whispering in my ear. 'I'm sure we could make our own entertainment.'

I shuddered, giving him my very best disdainful look. He'd obviously learnt his seduction skills from a Carry On film.

'Come on, they'll be wondering where we've got to. And, besides, you've got a job to do!'

'Good grief, woman, you're such a spoilsport. Come on, then. The sooner we get this over, the better, as far as I'm concerned.'

Well, at least we agreed on one thing. If Jimmy

had been here in place of Barney, I just knew it
would have been a totally different experience.
Jimmy went out of his way to make everyone
around him feel comfortable and at ease. And to
think that I would have been getting to know a very
different version of the Jimmy I now knew. Goosebumps ran the length of my arms.

Back at our table, I was relieved when Janine
managed to engage Barney in conversation. I was
much happier chatting to Simon and his wife, Han-
nah, hearing about their plans for their forthcoming holiday rather than Barney's self-obsessed
mutterings.

And aside from the small matter of Barney, the
evening was turning out to be a great success. The
chef at the Langton Hotel was Michelin starred and
his menu of watercress soup, followed by a fricassee
of black leg chicken, young leeks and cream of
morels was deliciously sublime.

By the time we'd finished our trio of puddings –
passion fruit and mango cheesecake, a chocolate
brownie and a clotted cream ice cream concoction –
a buzz of excitement was building around the room

in anticipation of the highlight of the evening, the charity auction.

I'd been a bit worried about Barney because he'd been throwing back the champagne like it was going out of fashion, but I needn't have done. As soon as he stood up, the professional entertainer in him took over, and within seconds he had the entire crowd eating out of his hand.

'Firstly, I'd like to thank Merron Enterprises for asking me to be a part of this magnificent event. I am delighted to be here, especially honoured to be standing here tonight in place of our much-loved, recently departed Jimmy Mack.' A respectful ripple of applause resonated around the room. 'Please raise your glasses, ladies and gentlemen, to someone I was proud to call my friend, Mr Jimmy Mack.'

Barney looked me straight in the eye as he lifted his glass, a smile resting on his lips. And I knew then that everything Jimmy had said about Barney had been true. He was a complete fake – insincere and dishonest and, in the brief time I'd spent with him, I'd come to see both sides of his big personality. I felt a pang of disloyalty to Jimmy for even being here with Barney. The audience might have been swayed by his display of affection for his recently departed colleague, but I knew it was all just an act, like Jimmy had warned.

I was relieved when the auction was underway. Begrudgingly, I had to admit that Barney was very good at his job. From the first lot, he whipped up the interest of the audience and the bids flowed in from the off. Dinner for two at a top London restaurant, a weekend for two in Paris, tickets to a top theatre show, a Chanel handbag; the items came thick and fast, and if there was ever a lull in the proceedings, Barney enthusiastically stirred up the audience, eliciting as many bids as he could, which was exactly what he'd been hired to do. This year, the proceeds from the auction were being divided between a local children's hospice and a drugs and alcohol rehabilitation centre, so every penny really did count.

'Fantastic,' said Simon, in my ear. 'We're already well into five figures. At this rate, we're going to easily surpass last year's total. Barney was definitely the right man for the job.'

'Yes, wasn't he?' I said, trying to match his enthusiasm. I couldn't help feeling, though, that I was betraying Jimmy's memory. Bringing the hammer down on the final lot to enthusiastic applause, Barney stepped down from the stage and joined us back at the table. As the band started playing, he held out his hand towards me.

'I think it's in my contract that I can choose to have the first dance with the most beautiful woman in the room. Isn't that right, Simon?' He smiled at me as my boss nodded his agreement and I was aware of everyone's eyes upon us.

'I'd be delighted to,' I said, walking onto the dance floor with a fixed grin upon my face, the muscles in my body rigid with tension, knowing I didn't have any choice in the matter. I was thankful, at least, that it was an up-tempo number and not a slow smoochy one. Soon we were joined by loads of other revellers, bopping to the music. The band rocked, playing a succession of old classics, which kept everyone up on their feet. When I thought I was about to collapse in a heap on the floor, I made my excuses to Barney.

'Crikey,' I gasped. 'I'm so out of shape. I'm going to have to sit down.'

'Let me come with you,' said Barney, laughing. 'And rest assured, young lady, you are in very decent shape.' He ran his hand down my arm, pulling me close to his side. 'Another bottle of champagne?' he asked, summoning the attention of a passing waiter.

Back at the table, he topped up my glass, edging his chair closer to mine again. The rest of our group was up on the floor, bopping, and I was glad of the chance to sit back and watch them all enjoying themselves. Barney, though, seemed intent on focusing all his attention on me.

'You have beautiful eyes,' he said, leaning over and running a fingertip down my cheek. 'A beautiful smile.' His finger touched my lips. 'And beautiful breasts,' he added with glee as his gaze returned to the spot where it had been focused most of the night.

I gave him a withering look, not trusting myself to say anything. I wished someone would come over and rescue me or talk to Barney and distract his attention, but everybody seemed to be giving us a very wide berth. When he leant over and planted a wet kiss on my cheek, I nearly fainted in surprise.

'Aaargh!' I yelped, feeling a hand grab my inner thigh. 'Barney! Stop it! Now, if you'll excuse me, I just need to pop to the loo. Again. It's all that champagne,' I said, with a forced smile.

'Don't be long,' he chuckled, as I stumbled out of my seat. 'I'll be waiting for you!'

Threading my way through the tables, I was aware of the knowing glances and sidelong smirks coming my way. Pete, one of the sales team, grabbed me by the arm as I walked past.

'Alice, you seem to be getting on famously with Barney. You and him an item now? Remember us when you're on the cover of *Hello!* magazine, won't you?' I scowled, but it did nothing to stop the sniggering from the occupants of the table.

'Just drop it, Pete,' I snapped, more viciously than I intended. 'I'm only doing my job and Barney Roberts is definitely not my idea of the perfect date.'

'Ooh-er, sorry, Alice. We were only joking, we didn't mean anything by it. Honest.'

I pushed aside the chair in my way and waltzed off, their laughter ringing after me.

Outside, I glanced at my watch. It was 11.45.

From memory, Barney's taxi had been booked for 12.30 a.m., so I only had another three-quarters of an hour of this torment to endure. Hopefully, by the time I got back to the table, he'd be busy in conversation with someone else.

I wandered outside, the rush of cold air taking my breath away, but after the crushing claustrophobia of the function room, it was a welcome sensation. Rubbing my hands up my arms to ward off the cold, I paced up and down for as long as my goosebumped skin could bear, which was only a matter of minutes, before heading back inside.

'Aha, so this is where you've been hiding?' There really was no escaping this man.

'Crikey, it's blooming freezing out there,' I said, my teeth chattering.

'Here, let me warm you up.' Manoeuvring me into a small passageway to the side of the cloakroom, he threw his arms around me, pushing his body hard up against me, his lips pressed firmly against mine. I shuddered with revulsion, what exactly was that prodding me? I wriggled beneath his boozy breath, using all my strength to push him away, but he was far too strong and soon his tongue was probing my mouth, his large hands lunging down my top.

'Stop it, Barney!' With a force I didn't know I possessed, I slipped out from under his embrace. 'What the hell do you think you're doing?' My breath was coming in short sharp spurts. 'I'm not interested in you in that way, okay? I've got a boyfriend, for heaven's sake!' I said, sounding like a virginal teenager.

'And I've got a wife. But I won't tell your boyfriend if you don't tell my wife.' Laughing, he grabbed me by the arm and spun me round to face him. 'Come on, darling, you've been teasing me all night in that luscious dress of yours. Let's not play games with each other.' His hand grasped my breast while the other hand drew my head in towards him. I squeezed my mouth shut and aimed my knee very firmly in the direction of his crotch.

'Hey, feisty!' His breath was ragged now. 'I like that in a woman.'

'Leave it, Barney!' I stormed away, smoothing my dress down over my hips, the sight of two huge ladders in my stockings only making my mood darker. Barney followed behind.

'What the...?' We said it in unison, both stopping on the spot, our eyes meeting in panic. An almighty gust of wind whipped through the foyer, as the twinkly lights of the chandeliers flashed on and off. All the doors leading off the lobby rattled open and shut. Instinctively, I looked towards the glass frontage of the hotel, thinking a juggernaut had crashed through the doors. Please, God, not a bomb! Not with all these people around.

'Shit!' Barney's brow creased as he looked one way and then the other, tucking in his shirt at the same time. 'What the hell was that?'

'I don't know.' Shivering, I looked around, stunned, as people filed out from the main hall to see what all the commotion was about. Goosebumps ran the length of my body. I wondered if I might be going down with something, I was that cold. What on earth was going on?

'Je-sus Christ!' came Barney's plaintive cry as suddenly he was lifted clean off his feet and catapulted into a nearby cheese plant.

'Are you okay?' I ran over, bending down to tend to him. I felt the air around me vibrating as Barney was lying spread-eagled on the floor, the mucky brown contents of the plant pot scattered over his previously pristine white shirt.

'Do I look bloody okay?' He wiped his forearm across his face, revealing a thunderous expression. He rolled over onto his front and pushed himself up onto his knees, pain shadowing his every movement. 'Someone just had a pop at me. Who the hell did that?'

'What?' I held out my arm for him as he struggled to his feet, but he pushed me aside, looking at me accusingly. 'No, Barney, no one had a pop at you. I was here by your side the whole time. I don't know what happened. I thought it was a bomb at first or an earthquake or something.' The words tumbled out as I looked around for an explanation.

Just as he pulled himself up to his full height, his legs buckled beneath him again and he collapsed back down on the floor. Sneers of derision were wafting our way.

'Well, it's hardly surprising, considering the amount of booze he's been throwing down his throat all night,' someone muttered unhelpfully from behind us.

'Bastard!' said another very familiar voice. 'It's nothing less than the creep deserves.'

There was no mistaking that voice, at all. I spun round on the spot.

'Jimmy!' Amongst the throng of partygoers in their dinner suits and glamorous dresses, Jimmy stood out like an angelic beacon in his scruffy jeans and T-shirt as he glowered, angelically, over the huddled figure on the floor, his mouth set firm, his eyes flaring with anger.

'Christ, woman!' Barney groaned from the floor. 'You could at least get my name right.' He struggled to his feet again, brushing away my attempts to help him up. 'I knew I should never have taken this job on. What a bloody waste of time. I'm out of here.'

'Did you do this?' I said through clenched teeth to Jimmy, who was shadowing Barney like a prize fighter going in for the final onslaught.

He shrugged and turned away, dropping his gaze to the floor.

'The guy's been out of order all night. Hassling you, coming on to you. Kissing you like that!' Indignation mixed with fury whirled around Jimmy in a cloud. 'It's not as though you didn't warn him. What did he expect? He had it coming.'

'Oh, Jimmy,' I whispered, reaching out a hand to touch him. 'You shouldn't have done this, though. Look at the state of him. I had it all under control.'

'Like hell you did! If I hadn't stepped in when I did, God knows what would have happened.' He pushed back his sleeves, as he paced the floor, looking as if he might jump on Barney again at any moment, and then folded his arms, defiantly.

I shook my head, hardly believing that Jimmy could have caused so much mayhem, but feeling secretly thankful that he had. Had he been watching over me all night, my very own guardian angel? It gave me a reassuring warm glow. As I looked over at him now, he gave me a sheepish smile and shrugged. Despite myself, I couldn't help but smile back.

'Come on, Barney,' I said, waving away the small crowd that had congregated in a huddled mass. 'I think your taxi's waiting outside. This is one night you won't forget in a hurry!'

17

I sat in Lexie's kitchen, mopping up chocolate brioche crumbs from an Emma Bridgewater plate, trying not to contemplate the events of the previous evening.

'Morning, Alice, how are you?'

The last thing I expected to see was a half-naked man wandering into the kitchen, helping himself to a banana from the fruit bowl and peeling it in a very provocative manner in front of me.

'Phil? Phil! Nice to see you again,' I spluttered, wiping my mouth clean with my fingers. 'How's things?' I struggled to keep my gaze fixed firmly on his face.

'Great, thanks.' He took a glass from the cupboard and placed it under the cold tap, looking very much at home. 'Don't worry,' he said apologetically. 'I'm not hanging around. I'm playing squash in half an hour.'

'Right, okay. No worries,' I said, wondering how long Lexie and Phil had been so well acquainted.

The sly little minx, I thought, helping myself to another chocolate brioche when Phil left the room. I'd known there'd been a bit of chemistry at work that night, but I had no idea that things had fast-forwarded to the staying over stage. Why hadn't she told me?

'What?' she said, coyly, from under long lashes, after she'd seen Phil out of the front door.

She gave a dismissive shrug of her shoulders, a self-indulgent smile resting on her lips.

'It's early days,' she said, looking sheepish, 'but I really like him, Alice. He seems such a genuine guy.'

'I'm sure he is,' I smiled, 'especially if he's a friend of Damon's. I just wish you'd warned me. I wasn't expecting to come across his half-naked form over my breakfast. It was a bit of a shock, that's all.'

She laughed, her whole being bathed in a glow of early love, or lust, more likely.

'Sorry, it wasn't planned. I didn't realise he would be here. It... um... just happened. You know what it's like.'

No, I didn't actually. Something like that hadn't happened in my little world for a long time, although weird, wacky and totally unexpected things of a celestial nature were becoming something of a regular occurrence.

'Hmmm, yeah. But I'm guessing that's not the reason why you insisted I came round here this morning. To give the once-over to your new boyfriend?'

'No, of course not.' She jumped up as if suddenly remembering and walked over to her desk. Unplugging her laptop, she gathered up the cable and brought it over to where I was sitting. 'I wanted you to see this,' she said, lifting the lid on the computer, her fingers flying over the keyboard, 'without Jimmy standing over us, giving us the benefit of his opinion.'

'Fair enough.' I didn't like to mention that Jimmy seemed to possess omnipresent powers and was probably watching over us this very moment. I didn't like to consider that thought too much myself.

'You'll never believe this. I was Googling Jimmy the other night...'

I raised my eyebrows.

'Yes. Just to see if I could find out some more background information on him. Something that would shed some clues as to why he's ended up in your life. You have to admit it's all a bit strange...'

Strange was putting it mildly.

'When I came upon this.' She loaded YouTube and clicked the 'play' button. She'd brought me round to her cottage on a Sunday morning to watch a video clip? 'It's an interview with Jimmy on one of those satellite channels.'

I recognised the interviewer, a woman in her late fifties with a neat blonde hairstyle and a warm lilting Irish accent who had rarely been off our TV screens a few years earlier, but nowadays was relegated to an afternoon chat show on one of the lesser-known channels.

'She's talking to Jimmy about his career,' she explained, fast-forwarding through the clip, 'but it's towards the end where it gets really interesting. Here!' she said, stopping the tape with a dramatic stab at the keyboard. 'Just look at this.'

'So, Jimmy, you've reached an unrivalled position in your career. You're the nation's number one TV presenter and your weekend radio show attracts listening figures that other DJs can only dream about. What's next for you? There have been rumours that you may be leaving our shores to cross the Atlantic.'

Jimmy shrugged in that half-committal way of his, the corners of his lips twitching upwards. It was a look I'd been on the end of on numerous occasions over the last few weeks, and seeing it practised on someone else, in another lifetime, stirred uncomfortable feelings.

'Is this something you'd consider? A move to the States?'

He paused, shifting in his chair, and examined the backs of his hands.

'To be honest with you, Margot, although I've had some very tempting offers, I wouldn't want to leave the UK. I love this country, it's my home and I feel very privileged to be doing the job that I do. As long as the great British public are prepared to tolerate my ugly mug on their screens, then I'm happy to stay and continue doing what I love doing best.'

A spontaneous round of applause rippled around the studio.

I looked over at Lexie and I was certain that I caught a tear in her eye to match the one in my own.

'And with such a busy working schedule, Jimmy, do you find any time to pursue a personal life? We hear very little about the private side to Jimmy Mack.'

'Well, to be honest, there isn't a great deal to tell.' He laughed lightly, running a hand through his dark hair. 'But it's something I'm very conscious of. The success, the fame and all the trimmings that come with this lifestyle mean nothing without someone special to share it with. And I'm a great romantic at heart.' He exchanged a flirtatious look with Margot. 'I believe there's someone out there for each of us, someone special, your soulmate if you like. I'm still looking for mine.'

'Jimmy, I'll be your special person!' A girl called out from the crowd, to the cheers of the audience. Jimmy and Margot joined in with the laughter.

'It's fair to say I won't die a happy man until I've met the woman I'm destined to spend the rest of my life with.'

A collective 'ahh' went round the crowd.

Margot shuffled her papers together and looked around, a satisfied smile upon her lips as she surveyed the rapt faces looking on.

'I think you may regret uttering those words, Jimmy. Your inbox will be overflowing with all sorts of propositions by tomorrow. It's been a pleasure talking to you, Jimmy. Thank you very much for your time.'

Lexie clicked on the screen, shutting down the programme, and turned to me as if she'd suddenly discovered the meaning of the universe.

'It's amazing, isn't it? Everything makes absolute sense now.'

'It does?' I muttered, still reeling from seeing Jimmy talking so candidly about his personal life.

'Yes! Didn't you hear what he said? That he wouldn't be able to die a happy man until he met the woman of his dreams, his soulmate. Don't you understand what it all means, Alice?' She closed the lid on the laptop and walked across to the window, before turning round to fix her gaze on me.

'No.' I shrugged. 'To be honest, I have no idea what it all means.'

'Alice, you must see. This whole thing hasn't been about Donna, that's just a complication. It's about you and Jimmy. You were meant to be together. As a couple. Soulmates. It's so romantic.' She clasped her hands in front of her, swooning. Clearly her night with Phil had brought out her latent sentimental side.

'You were destined to meet,' she went on. 'At the Charity Ball, no doubt. Until fate decided to put its ugly boot into the plans and kybosh the whole thing. And who knows what might have happened next?'

'Don't be ridiculous,' I said, unable to ignore the warm feeling of recognition in my stomach, thinking she was being anything but ridiculous.

'Marriage? Babies?' she continued. 'It was all written in the stars for you. It's just so sad that his future and, more importantly, your future have been snatched away. Just like that.' She clicked her fingers, making me sit up to attention. 'Jimmy's obviously got stuck here, living this strange existence, not willing to move over to the other side until he's spent some time with his true love. That's you.'

I stood up, quickly steadying myself with my hands on the table as my head swum in a disbelieving fog. I sat back down again, the blood rushing to somewhere below my knees.

'It's a bit of a leap, isn't it?' I stuttered. 'You're putting two and two together and getting five.'

'No, I'm not, Alice. It's the truth. And judging by your expression, you know it to be the truth too. Think about it. A larger-than-life ghost who can't be seen or heard by anyone else turns up in your life and shows no sign of moving on. It's the only plausible explanation.'

That's when I burst into tears. It was so utterly fanciful and yet completely logical to me too. Ever since that day in the field when I first met Jimmy, I'd been fighting feelings that had been threatening to swamp me. Now, I wasn't sure I could hold onto them a moment longer.

'Aw, Alice, I'm so sorry.' She wrapped her arms

around me. 'Trust you,' she said, shaking her head wryly, wiping the tears from my cheeks with a tissue. 'You finally get to meet the man of your dreams and he turns out to be not of this world. It could only happen to you.'

'It's not funny,' I said, sniffing back the tears, my stomach churning with the enormity of the situation.

'No, darling, it's not funny at all,' she spluttered, and we fell into each other's arms, our whole bodies shaking with laughter.

* * *

'You're cross with me, aren't you?'

It was later the same day and, after a few tumultuous hours spent round at Lexie's, alternating between fits of laughter and bouts of tears, I was back at home, attacking the ironing with a ferocity borne of complete muddle-headedness.

'What?' I flapped a work blouse in the air and fitted it across the board, the steam hissing from the iron matching my mood. Jimmy was sprawled across the sofa, surrounded by newspapers, coffee mugs and chocolate wrappers.

'You! Call me sensitive, but I think you've got the hump with me. Big time.'

I shook my head, grabbing a skirt from the basket.

'No, Jimmy, I'm not cross with you, I'm just...'

Well, what could I tell him? That my sister thought he was the love of my life and we'd been destined to spend the rest of our time together?

It sounded completely ridiculous, but no more ridiculous than Jimmy's theory about Donna. We'd been to see her and still there was no sign of Jimmy moving across. The world still thought Jimmy was the father of her baby and I was only too willing to believe that Jimmy was the love of my life. It was hopeless. There were no answers, only more and more questions.

Jimmy had gone and ruined everything by carelessly spinning his car off the road. How thoughtless of him. And where exactly do you begin with a conversation like that? Especially with Jimmy's reaction to consider, too. Would he laugh heartily, throw back his head and snort with derision? Or would he scoop me up in his arms, lay me on the bed and make sweet, sweet love to me?

There was so much living and loving to do and yet I'd fallen in love with a dead man. Sadness washed over me. I used to pride myself on my cool and collected thinking, but these days, my head was all over the place.

'Look, I know I shouldn't have hit him. That was out of order.' He held up his hands to me, looking suitably repentant. 'But I couldn't help myself. I was worried for you. I thought... well... when he put his hands all over your body like that... I just saw red... and... I'm sorry. Not that I hit him, but that you're upset.'

I sighed. Last night, all the kerfuffle with Barney, it seemed like a lifetime ago.

'The thought of that slimy toerag taking advantage of you, well, it was too much to bear.' He jumped up, swinging his long legs over the side of the sofa and took my hands from across the ironing board. 'I'm really sorry, Alice. I know I shouldn't have let it get to me like that. Am I forgiven? Please?'

I had no chance of staying annoyed with Jimmy

for any longer than a few nanoseconds. The softness of his gaze upon my face, the tilt of his head
and the corners of his mouth twitching in anticipation of that broad grin were enough for me to for-
give him anything. But I wasn't about to tell him
that.

'Well, you can't keep stepping into my life and
sorting out my problems for me. I mean, what
would I have done if you hadn't been around?'

'My point exactly!'

'Jimmy, stop it. You're not my guardian angel.
Soon you'll be on your way and then I'll have to sort
things out on my own.'

'Hmm, I suppose. Although I'd like to be able to
look after you forever. Maybe when I get to the
Main Place, I'll drop in at Heavenly Resources and
see if there are any vacancies for guardian angels.
Then I can spend the rest of eternity looking out for
you. I like the sound of that.' His fingers touched
my cheek as his eyes smiled at me, drawing me in
as they always did.

I laughed, shaking my head, my insides melting
at the thought of Jimmy being forever at my side.

'All right, all right, you're forgiven.' I folded the

last remaining item in the pile and flicked off the switch. 'Is it too early for a glass of something?' I said, looking at my watch. There was so much I wanted to say, but I didn't know where to begin. The idea of him looking after me forever was hugely romantic, but the suggestion felt like an un-expected body blow. It would never happen. Jimmy was just passing through.

'Thanks,' I said, gladly accepting the glass of Sauvignon Blanc he was offering, taking a welcome sip. 'How did you know I was in trouble, then?' Jimmy had the knack of turning up at exactly the right moment, or the wrong one, depending on how you looked at it. 'Are you constantly hovering around, taking note of everything that's going on?'

He shrugged and smiled.

'I know I'm awesome, but I'm not that awe-some.' His expression became serious. 'It's a feeling I get, Alice. Something that comes over me. I just know, in here,' he said, banging his chest with his fist, 'when you're anxious or afraid and then I have to come and see what I can do to help.'

'Really?'

'Yeah.' He nodded ruefully. 'And I'm sorry if I

overstep the mark at times, but I promise you I'm not some kind of spectral stalker, watching your every move from the shadows.'

I made a big show of shivering exaggeratedly.

'Thank goodness for that,' I said, joining him on the sofa with my glass of wine.

'Although that's not to say the temptation hasn't been there.'

'And what's that supposed to mean?' I elbowed him in the ribs as he shifted himself closer to me on the sofa.

'Well, let's just say that a less honourable heavenly being than myself might take advantage of their elevated position, using it to intrude on those special intimate moments, but obviously that's not something I would ever consider.'

I looked at him through narrowed eyes.

'You'd better not,' I said.

'Of course I wouldn't.' He laughed, looking as though he just might. 'I only hope you don't get into too much trouble at work because of my behaviour last night.' He picked up the remote control and pointed it at the telly. The familiar soothing opening bars to *Endeavour* wafted over us. It wasn't too much of a leap of the imagination to think that we were like any other couple enjoying a night in front of the telly.

'Don't worry about that,' I said, settling comfortably back into the sofa and into Jimmy's arms, feeling anything was possible with him at my side. 'I'm sure it won't be anything I can't handle.'

18

And really, it wasn't, although my popularity ranking had risen twentyfold by Monday morning and I had a whole succession of casual visitors at my desk, wanting the lowdown on what exactly had gone on between Barney and me on the night of the auction, but I batted each of them away.

'So, did you go back to his place after the ball?'

'No, I most certainly didn't!'

'Do you think Barney's an alcoholic?'

'No.'

'So why did he end up sprawled on the floor?'

'It was an unfortunate accident.'

'Did he make a pass at you?'

'No.'

'Do you think he's a sex addict?'

'How the hell would I know?'

'Do you like Barney?'

'I think he did an excellent job as auctioneer.'

'Do you think Barney will sue us?'

'No.'

'Do you think the company will sue Barney?'

'Of course not.'

I'd already taken a telephone call from Barney's agent first thing to say that in the event of any members of the press making enquiries about his client's attendance at the Charity Ball, we were to keep shtum and refer them to him. I quickly confirmed that our discretion was assured and fired off an email to the relevant departments to the same effect. Barney Roberts and his entourage clearly didn't want any bad publicity, but then again, neither did Merron Enterprises.

I penned a handwritten note to Barney, thanking him for his sterling job – after all, he had helped raise in excess of £20,000 for our charities and that's what he'd been hired for – and sent him a huge bouquet of flowers for his efforts. I was hoping that would be an end to the matter.

My tummy grumbling in protest at the lack of breakfast, I glanced at my watch and decided to pop out at lunchtime for a walk and a sandwich. I'd just picked up my jacket when the phone buzzed into action again.

'Alice, it's reception here. There's a Miss Smith to see you. She doesn't have an appointment but is very insistent that she sees you. She says it's important.'

Sighing, I slipped my jacket off my shoulders and hung it back on the coat stand. A journalist, I didn't doubt, with the scent of a juicy story wafting beneath her nostrils. Who, I wondered, had tipped her off?

'Tell her I'm busy.' I drummed my fingernails on the desk. 'Could you give her my card and ask her to contact me by email or telephone to make an appointment?'

Debbie lowered her voice to a whisper at the other end of the telephone.

'I've already tried that, but she's refusing to leave. She says she's happy to wait until you're free.

I've explained it could be some time.' The frustration in Debbie's voice wafted down the line. Our most experienced receptionist, she'd been with the company for years and was used to dealing with all sorts of people and situations. Obviously, this visitor was being particularly troublesome. 'I've asked if she would like to speak to someone else, maybe the Press Office, but she's adamant that she talks to you.'

'Okay,' I sighed. 'Ask her to take a seat, I'll be down in a moment.'

I scrabbled around on the desk and found the piece of paper with the telephone number of Barney's agent. Whatever information Miss Smith thought she was sitting on was not going to be confirmed by me, that was for sure. But how exactly had this woman got hold of my name? It had to be one of my so-called friends or colleagues from the ball the other night.

Downstairs, I walked through the double doors that led into reception, breathing in sharply, and marched across to the plush leather sofas. I took one look at the pitiful creature dressed in a grey tracksuit who was sitting huddled on one end of the sofa, examining the backs of her hands, and faltered. This couldn't be the hard-nosed journalist I was expecting, surely? I turned to the reception desk and Debbie answered my unasked question with a nod and a shrug.

'Miss Smith?' I said, brightly.

She was no more than a girl with mousey hair and a smattering of freckles, yet her features were strangely familiar.

'Alice, hi, thanks so much for seeing me.' Her face lit up, but even her welcoming smile couldn't mask the exhaustion in her eyes. 'Sorry about just turning up like this. I did try phoning, but... well, I've never been very good on the phone.'

'Donna?' I stuttered. The voice, much less assertive than when I'd last heard it was unmistakable, although the unkempt hair and blotchy complexion made her completely unrecognisable from the blonde bombshell I'd met in the club that night. 'I'm sorry, I didn't realise it was you.'

She gave a wry smile.

'That was the general idea.' She ran a hand through her lacklustre hair, and I noticed her fingernails were bitten ragged. 'I left the wig at home.'

I tried to hide my gasp of surprise. She looked so different, much more ordinary without all the bling, yet still so pretty in a completely washed-out and weary manner. I couldn't help but feel sorry for her.

'Shall we go and grab a drink?' I suggested.

'Um, I'd rather not. You know, just in case someone spots me looking like this. Is there somewhere else we can go here, somewhere more private?' The brashness that had been so apparent in the nightclub had been replaced by a beguiling softness.

'Yes, yes, of course. Hang on a minute.' I got up and walked over to Debbie, who'd been watching us the whole time from behind her desk. 'Is there a meeting room free?'

'Room 2B on the ground floor?'

'Great. Could you book it out for me, please? And arrange some tea and sandwiches?'

Debbie was already busy tapping into her keyboard.

'I'll get straight onto it,' she said.

'Come on,' I said to Donna, 'follow me.'

No sooner had we closed the door of the

meeting room and settled ourselves into our chairs than Donna turned to me.

'I wanted to apologise. For the other night.' She undid the zip on her hoodie, displaying her burgeoning bump, and settled into her chair, immediately looking more relaxed. 'It was just such a shock, that's all. I wasn't expecting it.'

'Yes, I suppose it must have been. And I'm sorry for hijacking you like that when you were on a night out, but it was the only way we could think of getting to meet you. And my sister Lexie can be a bit over-enthusiastic at times.' I paused. 'How's it going?' I asked, nodding towards her tummy.

'Fine,' she said, her face lighting up. 'I've just about got used to the idea now and at least the sickness has stopped. I know I look a wreck, but actually I'm feeling a lot better than I've done in weeks.' She paused, dropping her gaze to the floor. 'It's been a difficult time.'

Just then, there was a knock at the door and Debbie appeared bearing a tray.

'Many thanks, just leave it on the table here. Tea?' I offered to Donna, picking up the pot and pouring the piping hot liquid.

'Thanks. And I'll have a couple of sandwiches, if you don't mind.' She helped herself to a handful, piling them on her plate. 'I've been absolutely ravenous ever since I became pregnant. Talk about eating for two. I think I'm eating for an entire rugby team.'

I laughed, still trying to reconcile the two completely disparate images of Donna that were jostling for position in my head. There was no sign of the meticulously groomed, hard-edged career girl who would do anything to get herself into the limelight, who I'd seen a glimpse of the other week, in the young woman who sat in front of me now.

'I suppose you know why I'm here?' she said, between mouthfuls of egg and cress sandwich.

I shook my head. To be honest, I hadn't given it any thought. I'd been so keyed up about having to deal with some awkward questions from a newspaper hack that coming face to face with Donna's alter ego had been at first a shock and then a relief.

'I did a lot of thinking after that night,' she began. 'You really brought things home to me. About the baby and what... and what I've done.' Her shoulders slumped and tears gathered in her eyes.

She stood up, brushing crumbs away from her bump, before sitting back down again. 'How could I have been so stupid?'

I shook my head in response.

'I don't know what possessed me to come up with the whole thing in the first place. It just seemed like a good idea. And, of course, as soon as I mentioned Jimmy's name, the tabloids were over me like a rash. And then, well, I was in far too deep. I couldn't get out of it.'

It was almost too much to believe that Donna was sitting in front of me, confessing that Jimmy wasn't the father of her child, after all. I felt like punching the air with my fist. Wait until I tell Lexie, I thought excitedly. And what about Jimmy? Was he hovering about us, doing a ghostly jig?

'So, um, do you know who the father is?'

She lifted her eyes to me and the laser-like glare of Donna Diamond, the celebrity, bore down on me.

'Of course I know who the father is! Everyone has this impression of me, that I'm a real slapper, but I promise you, I'm not.' She shook her head, smiling wryly. 'I've been with my boyfriend Tony for years. He's a doorman at Marko's. And then we split up just before I found out I was pregnant and I didn't know what to do, how I would ever cope alone? I didn't dare tell Tony. I thought he wouldn't want to know me. That I'd deliberately trapped him. He always said he never wanted children.' She shrugged, as if she could barely make sense of it all herself. 'I'm really sorry about Jimmy. You know, him being a friend of yours and everything. It must have been awful reading those things about him.' She dropped her gaze, looking apologetic. 'I met him once.'

'Did you?' Of course, I knew they'd met. Jimmy had told me all about it, but now I wanted to hear it from her side.

'Not long before he died. At a black tie function. He seemed really nice. A proper gentleman. Most men look at me in a certain way. But not Jimmy. He wasn't interested in me in that way at all. I thought then what a lovely husband and dad he'd make. You were lucky to have him as your friend.'

'Yeah,' I said wistfully. 'I think he may be the best friend I've ever had.'

She tilted her head to one side, a questioning

expression on her face.

'I mean I was lucky to have him as a friend.' I clasped my cup in my hands. 'I haven't really got used to him not being around any more.'

'Yeah, it must be hard. Were you like a proper couple, together?'

'No, not in that way. Although...' I sighed, my gaze shifting to the window. Although what? We were just building up to it? We would have been together if he hadn't gone and got himself killed? I could hardly tell that to Donna.

'Ah, that's a shame.' Her face shone with sincerity. 'I think you would have made a really lovely couple.'

'Thanks.' I poured us another cup of tea, feeling a flush of heat to my cheeks. Hurriedly, I changed the subject. 'So what did Tony say when you finally told him?'

'Well, I didn't, that was the thing. He read about it in the papers and he was furious, absolutely furious. Wanted to go round there and then and knock Jimmy's lights out, but obviously it was too late for that. I'm sorry,' she said, quickly realising what she'd said.

'No, don't worry, it's okay.'

She combed her hands through her hair. Her every move was accentuated with weariness.

'It was awful, really bad. I had to convince Tony that I hadn't slept with Jimmy and we had lots of rows and sleepless nights over it all, but I think,' she held her crossed fingers up in the air, 'that we've sorted things out now.'

'That's good,' I said. 'So you're going to make a go of it, then?'

'Yeah. Funny thing is, Tony's made up about the baby, really thrilled. I've told him we can have a DNA test done once the baby's born if he wants to, but I know for certain he's the father, there just hasn't been anyone else.'

'I'm pleased,' I said, meaning it, although it didn't get over the small matter of the whole of the nation still believing Jimmy Mack to be the father of Donna's unborn child. Her confession might go some way to making me feel better, but I didn't think it would make any difference to Jimmy, knowing his reputation had been sullied.

'I can't wait to be a mum,' beamed Donna. 'It's what I've always wanted, and it means a brand-new start for us.' She flashed the biggest diamond I'd ever seen on her left hand. 'Tony's asked me to marry him.'

'Really! That's great news. Congratulations, Donna.' I was thrilled for them both, but why had she gone to all the effort of coming to see me and telling me?

'The exciting thing is that Rex Stafford has negotiated a deal with *Ciao* magazine for us. They're going to do a huge twelve-page spread on us, with photos of Tony and me at home, explaining the whole story. You know, why we split up, how I fell pregnant, the reason I made up the story about Jimmy. It's going to be a huge exclusive. There's even talk about a follow-up television series. Wheee!' she cried, rubbing her hands together gleefully. 'We could be the new Katie and Peter.'

And look what happened to them, I thought, electing to keep that to myself, not wanting to spoil Donna's moment.

'That's fantastic,' I gushed, the revelation that Jimmy's name would be cleared after all uppermost in my mind. 'So you're really going to admit that you made up the story about Jimmy?'

'I have to. For Tony's sake and for the sake of our future together. I want to wipe the slate clean and start all over again.'

Jimmy's name would be cleared, after all. His reputation wouldn't be sullied. This was what we'd been working so hard to achieve. What we'd both wanted. Now there would be nothing stopping Jimmy from passing over. I should have felt elated, but a cold pang of dread enveloped me.

I looked across at Donna, marvelling at her bravery. There was no way I would want to be in her shoes.

'Well, I think that's brilliant news, Donna, and I'm so pleased you've told me. I know all of Jimmy's family will be relieved to know the truth. I'll definitely look out for your story in the magazine.' I glanced at my watch, desperate now to tell Lexie and Jimmy the news, but I was also conscious of the fact that I needed to get back to my desk and do some work.

'Thanks for everything, Alice, for being so understanding.' She zipped up her hoodie and picked up her bag from the floor. 'There was just one other thing. Something I'm hoping you can help me with.'

'Okay,' I said tentatively. 'What is it?'

She screwed up her mouth, biting on her lip, her eyes flickering uneasily.

'Your sister, Lexie, is it?'

I nodded.

'She mentioned that you had psychic powers, that you could get in touch with the other side?'

'Oh well, I'm not really...'

'The thing is, I know I shouldn't have done it, but ever since I made up that story about Jimmy, funny things have been going on at home. Really funny things.' She shivered and I saw fear in her eyes. 'My house is haunted, Alice. No, really, it is,' she added, seeing my startled expression. 'It's dead creepy. It's almost got to the stage where I dread going home at night and I don't know what to do about it. How to get rid of it. I feel like I'm being punished for my lies. Is that something you can do, Alice? Get rid of ghosts?'

I took a sharp intake of breath. 'Well, I've had a little experience of that sort of thing,' I muttered, wondering if I should put an ad in the local paper, advertising my skills. Clearly there was a call for this type of service, although my success rate to date had hovered around the zero mark. In this case, though, I had a sneaky suspicion I might have more success.

'What sort of stuff has been going on, then?' I asked, warily.

'All sorts. You wouldn't believe it. The photos on my mantelpiece get changed around on a daily basis, the contents of my knicker drawer were swapped with the tea towel drawer, the lights flicker on and off of their own accord, but the worse thing of all is the weird sensations that go on around me.'

'Really?' I said, believing every single word of it.

'Yeah, it's seriously freaky, like someone blowing in my ear or tickling me with a feather duster. It drives me crazy. Tony thinks it's all in my mind because it never seems to happen when he's around, but I know I'm not imagining it, Alice, and I just want it all to stop. I can't live like this any more. I feel like I'm going mad. Do you think you'll be able to help?'

'Hmmm, I'm not sure, it sounds like you've got a particularly mischievous type of ghoul there. Some ghosts are more difficult to get rid of than others, but I could give it a try.'

'Would you?' Donna jumped up, surprising me by throwing her arms around me. 'I'd be ever so grateful. What would you need to do? Come round and perform a leaving ceremony or something? I've got a whole cupboard full of candles if you need them.'

'Well, I don't think that will be necessary, not in the first place, anyway. Leave it with me and I'll consult my special book at home and, er, um, I'll put together a magic spell. A special one. That should do the trick.'

'A spell? Isn't that what witches do?'

'Er, yes, obviously, but we sometimes use them in our line of work too. In those particularly tricky cases. Like this one.'

'I see,' said Donna, looking at me doubtfully. 'Well, if you could do whatever it is you need to do, I'd be ever so grateful.'

'Don't worry,' I said, standing up and reaching for the door handle. 'I'm extremely confident that I'll be able to sort out your unwelcome visitor once and for all.'

19

Sitting on the train on the way home from work that day – my car was in the garage for its MOT – I did something I'd never done before.

'Jimmy!' I cried very loudly in my head, banging my fist down on the seat next to me.

Even I was impressed when seconds later the man himself slipped into the space next to me and gave me the benefit of his broad grin.

'Hi, babe, receiving you loud and clear.'

Ignoring the fact that he was looking as louche and obscenely sexy as one ghost was possible to look, I turned on him.

'Don't you "babe" me, you despicable lowlife,

you! How you could do something like that is beyond me. It's despicable, completely despicable.'

'Uh-oh,' he said, sitting up in the seat and
leaning his face into mine, 'what have I done now?'

'As if you don't know!' I shook my head, barely
able to find the words. Interfering in my life was
one thing, but taking advantage of a poor defence-
less pregnant woman was something else entirely.

He held up his hands in the air sheepishly.

'No, I'm sorry, you'll have to give it to me
straight.'

'Don't you play the innocent with me.' I glared
at him through narrowed eyes. 'I had a visit today
from a certain Donna Diamond.'

'Oh,' said Jimmy, grimacing. He shifted uneasily
in his seat, screwing his mouth up on one side. 'I
see.'

'So what was all that stuff you were spouting
about not abusing your position? Not taking advantage of your ghostly powers? How you would never
do that sort of thing. Had a change of mind, did you?'

He winced and shrugged.

'Well, I just thought...'

'She's pregnant, for goodness' sake, Jimmy. I don't know what you were thinking. Going round there and scaring her witless, anything could have happened.'

'I didn't think,' said Jimmy, looking contrite, 'nothing has happened, has it?'

'No, it hasn't, but that's no thanks to you. The poor girl is completely exhausted, unable to sleep at nights and frightened for her life after all your antics. I'm surprised at you, Jimmy, for sinking so low.'

He slunk down in his seat, looking suitably guilty.

'Well, what was I supposed to do? Go to my grave with everyone thinking I was the father of her child? It might seem trivial to you, but it's my reputation on the line. I couldn't let it happen. I thought you'd understand that. You and Lexie didn't make any progress with Donna, so I thought I'd have a go.' He hunched his shoulders, frowning at the floor.

I shifted in my seat, turning my body away, and stared out of the window. The little-boy-lost treatment was wasted on me tonight. I couldn't believe how selfishly he'd behaved.

'I'm sorry, Alice,' he said, laying a hand on my arm. 'I thought a little gentle coercion might make her come to her senses,' he said quietly.

'Some gentle coercion? You've turned the girl into a gibbering wreck. She thinks she's upset the local chapter of Ghosts R Us and she sat in my office today, begging me for help.' I looked across at him as he kicked the heel of his red Converse into the seat like a schoolboy who'd been caught out but hadn't quite come to terms with his misdemeanour. 'She seems to think I've got special psychic abilities and has enlisted my help to sort you out. Somehow, I've become responsible for all of this. Honestly, Jimmy, you can be so infuriating at times.'

'Well, you have got special talents. You can speak to me, can't you? That's pretty impressive in anyone's book. Maybe you could develop this new-found skill into a career. You know, set up as a con-ciliatory service between the living and the recently departed. I think it could be a niche business.'

'Do you have to turn everything into a joke?'

'I'm sorry, Alice, really I am. I didn't mean any

harm by it. I suppose I didn't really think it through. But I promise,' he gave me a three fingered salute and smiled, 'dib dib dib, dob dob dob, I won't do any more haunting, well, not in Donna's direction, anyway.'

'You'd better not, Jimmy. Or in anyone else's direction, come to that. I've promised her I'll sort out the night-time visitations. She's a pregnant young woman who's got a chance of happiness with a man who loves her. You mustn't go spoiling it for her.'

'Oh, well, excuse me if I'm not beside myself with joy at Donna's good news. And when did you suddenly start fighting her corner, anyway? I thought you were on my side.' He slunk back down in his seat again.

The train rattled through station after station, its repetitive chanting motion strangely comforting.

I sighed, shaking my head as I turned to look at him.

'It's not that I'm taking sides, Jimmy, it's just that I've got to know Donna and I can see that underneath that harsh exterior, she's a really sweet girl. And she's sorry for what she's done to you. Really sorry. But hopefully she can put that right now.'

Jimmy rolled his eyes and sat forward in his seat.

'That's absolutely fine, then. Let's forget the fact that she's dragged my name through the mud. We can all pretend this whole thing never happened.'

'She's getting married, Jimmy. Isn't that lovely news?'

'Terrific,' he said, with more than a hint of sarcasm.

'No, it is, Jimmy, if you think about it. For them and for us. Donna and Tony are doing an exclusive with one of the big magazines and they're going to tell their whole story. And I mean the whole story. Tony's the father of Donna's baby and they both want the world to know that. It means your name will be cleared, after all.'

'Are you serious?'

'Absolutely. It's brilliant news, isn't it?'

'Yes, I guess.'

Just then a burly, bald man with a laptop case, a rucksack and several carrier bags shuffled his way in front of us and plonked his bags on the overhead rail.

'Excuse me, love, do you mind if I sit here?'

'No, that's fine,' I said, hiding a snigger as I clocked Jimmy's outraged expression.

'Humph! Some people are so rude,' he said, shaking his head, his eyes wide in indignation.

The man edged backwards to park his ample backside beside me and quickly jumped straight back up again, gasping in surprise as he turned to look at the seat accusingly.

'Are you okay?' I asked.

'Um, yes, I think so.' He stroked the upholstery gingerly with his hand. 'Just got an electric shock from the seat.'

'Ouch,' I said in understanding. 'I hate it when that happens.'

'Yeah, me too.' The man settled back down into his seat and flapped his newspaper noisily in the air.

'Well, what does he expect if he goes around pinching other people's seats? There's only one thing for it,' Jimmy said, landing in my lap and dangling his legs over the side of the seat. 'I'll have to come and sit with you.'

'Ooh-er,' I squealed, shifting myself along the cushion to make room for him.

'Not you too?' the man asked, raising his eyebrows.

'Must be something in the air,' I gasped, secretly grateful to the man. Now I could spend the rest of the journey snuggled in Jimmy's embrace, my head resting on his chest, my mind entertaining all sorts of heavenly possibilities.

20

Later that night, against my better judgement, I was sitting in the Plume of Feathers on the High Street, one part of a team of four competing in the weekly quiz.

I hated spending any time away from Jimmy, knowing it was precious time that we would never get back again, but Lexie had begged me to come along and, as Jimmy was off visiting his parents again, he came down firmly on my sister's side, insisting that a night out doing something ordinary would do no end of good.

We were first timers, but all the other tables

were crammed with what looked like very serious quizzer types.

'The band JLS have reformed in recent years, but what do the initials JLS stand for?' called the Quizmaster over the low rumble of the participants.

I looked across at Damon, who gazed vacantly at Phil, who shrugged at Lexie, who looked back at me, and then we all groaned in unison.

'No idea,' sighed Damon. 'I was banking on you lot knowing the popular culture questions. Come on, guys, you must know this one.'

'Well, maybe we can work it out,' Phil said, picking up his pencil and scribbling the letters down. 'Maybe it's the group members' names, like Jake, Luke, Simon, that kind of thing.'

I rolled my eyes. It clearly wasn't my fault that I'd teamed up with a group of numpties.

'Duh!' said Lexie, helpfully, putting into words my thoughts. 'There's four of them in the group and I know one's called Aston and one's called something like Marvin, so it can't be that.'

Phil threw his pencil onto the table.

'Well, at least I'm trying to come up with some

answers. You lot have been spectacular failures. I'm going to the bar.' Lexie and I exchanged a look and I bit on my lip to stop myself from giggling. 'Who wants another drink?'

'Good idea,' said Damon, looking only too eager to join him.

'So, I've been dying to ask. How's it all going? How's life with the most eligible ghost on the block?' Lexie leant over the table, looking at me expectantly. 'Any progress on that front?'

'Well, actually, yes.' I leant forward to meet her, looking over my shoulder just to make sure no one was listening in on our conversation. 'I've been meaning to tell you, but I didn't want to do it over the phone. You'll never guess who turned up at work?'

'Who?' Lexie asked, her eyes wide.

'Donna Diamond, that's who! Can you believe it?'

'Really? The cheek of the woman. What did she want? She didn't have her lawyers in tow, did she?'

'No, nothing like that. I think our little visit that night might have done the trick. She's decided to come clean about the baby. She's doing an exclusive with one of the big celebrity magazines. Donna and her future husband, Tony.'

Lexie clapped her hands together delightedly.

'You're kidding me! I don't believe it.' Lexie tidied her hair, which, after its recent psychedelic stage, she'd allowed to revert to its natural golden colour, making her look much softer, more feminine. 'I didn't like to say anything at the time, but I felt certain she wouldn't change her story. She seemed like a really tough cookie. I wonder what made her change her mind?'

I finished off the wine in my glass and lowered my voice.

'Well, I think sharing her house with a ghost these last couple of weeks may have had something to do with it.'

'Not Jimmy?' Lexie sniggered, looking over my head through the throng of people. 'He didn't! No wonder she caved in. I know what it's like to be on the end of his schoolboy pranks and it's no laughing matter. Still, I bet he's relieved. He must be over the moon that she's decided to see sense at last.'

'Yeah, he's delighted.' I paused looking around

the room. 'I'm just glad we got it all sorted out in the end. I couldn't have done it without you, Lexie.'

'What are sisters for?' she asked with that impish smile. She took hold of my hand from across the table and gave it a squeeze. 'So I reckon it won't be long now, then?'

There was a rush of groans mixed with pre-celebration cheers from the other tables as the end of the contest was announced.

'What won't?' I asked Lexie, momentarily distracted.

'Before Jimmy moves on.' She held my gaze. 'I suppose he had an incentive to stay all the time he was unfairly portrayed in the press, but now that's been sorted, there's nothing really to keep him here. Is there? I mean, he's found you and even if you're not prepared to admit it, he must now realise the reason why you two were thrown together. I'm sure it's only a matter of time before he goes on to his rightful place.'

'Oh, Lexie, how can we know? It's all pointless speculation. I had no idea Jimmy was going to turn up in my life or the reason why and I have no idea when he'll be leaving. To be honest, I haven't given it any thought.'

'Bollocks!' Lexie said rather too loudly, eliciting a disapproving glance from the team of 'Bright Sparks' on the next table. 'He's all you talk about, Alice. I'm only saying this because I'm worried about you. You're investing far too much time and emotional energy in Jimmy. And for what? He's a ghost for... for heaven's sake!' She laughed half-heartedly at her own joke. 'You're putting your life on hold for someone who's... who's... not even real.'

'I don't mind,' I said weakly. 'And besides, Jimmy is real to me.'

'I know you don't mind! But what happens when it all ends? Which it will. And soon, I don't doubt. You'll come crashing down to earth with a bang and you'll be left with what? Nothing. That's what.'

'Right, thanks,' I said, sitting back in my chair, folding my arms crossly. Just because she was acting out love's young dream with Phil, it didn't give her the right to tell me what I should be doing in my life and who I should be doing it with. I let out a heavy sigh. 'Thanks a lot, Lexie. I was having a nice evening till you started having a go at me.'

She reached over again and grabbed my wrists.

'I'm not having a go, but you must realise there's no future for you and Jimmy. You have to see that. You're in love with a dead man, a spook. And where can that possibly lead? Marriage, babies, a future? None of that's going to happen, Alice, and you're only building up a whole lot of hurt for yourself.'

My throat constricted and tears welled in my eyes as I furiously blinked them away, picking up my empty glass and swirling the dregs around the bottom. In love with Jimmy? I thought I'd done a pretty good job at hiding that from Lexie, and from Jimmy, but however hard I tried, there was no way I could deceive myself any longer. I'd known it almost from the very first day I met him. I didn't care about the future. I was happy where I was. In the here and now. With Jimmy at my side. For however long it might last.

'All the time you're holed up in that flat with your ghostly best friend, you're never going to meet anyone here in the real world. Someone like Damon, for instance. Why don't you give him a chance instead? He clearly thinks the world of you and yet you treat him like... like he's nothing.'

'So did we win, then?'

As if on cue, Damon returned, placing two glasses of wine down on the table, his deep brown eyes observing me thoughtfully.

I knew what Lexie was saying, but the truth was I didn't want anything or anyone in my life other than Jimmy.

'Thanks,' I said, smiling back at him. 'We came a close last, I think,' I added.

'Aw, well, there's always next month, I suppose. I'll do some heavy-duty swotting up before then, see if we can climb our way up the league tables.'

I laughed, but hurt bled through my veins. Next month? Would Jimmy even still be here then, I wondered sadly.

21

The following day, I left work early, jumped into the car and pulled back the roof. We were in the midst of a long glorious dry spell with uncharacteristically warm sunshine and blue cloudless skies. As I drove out of the car park, I decided, on a whim, not to turn left at the roundabout onto the bypass that led to home, but instead I took the right-hand turn and headed out of town along the Amerway Road. As I hummed away to the soothing tones of Michael Bublé, I was reminded of that first day when I met Jimmy. There was a similar stillness in the air, an intangible quality to the atmosphere, but instead of the wariness and trepidation that slowly crept over me then, this afternoon I felt only a sense of peace and contentment and something deep inside telling me that, in the end, everything would work out okay.

A couple of hours later, when I walked through the lychgate at the entrance to the churchyard, the same feeling engulfed me, wrapping itself around me like a big, fluffy comfort blanket.

'You'll be wanting to see James McArthur's grave, I wouldn't doubt.'

'Oh, hello.' I turned to see an old gentleman pushing a wheelbarrow overflowing with earth and wilting flowers. 'Yes, that's right. I was a friend of his. Do you have many visitors here, then?'

'Aye, we've had a few, these last few weeks.' He stopped, smiling wryly, gently easing himself into an upright position, and rested his hands on his haunches. 'Carry on along this path here, beyond the church and over in the left-hand corner of the churchyard, you'll find him.'

'Thanks,' I said, smiling.

It was a beautiful spot. The sound of birdsong rippled through the trees and in the neighbouring field, sheep grazed happily, oblivious to the famous celebrity who had recently moved in next door.

I wandered amongst the headstones, stopping to read some of the inscriptions, before reaching the spot where Jimmy had been laid to rest. It was too soon for his headstone to be in place, but the profusion of flowers marking his grave was testament to the loss felt by so many people.

I stood there for a few minutes, soaking up the atmosphere, at first not realising that tears were running freely down my cheeks as my eyes pored over the messages of condolence. Jimmy was just a memory to these people now and, although he was still very much part of my life, I knew it was only a matter of time before he was consigned to memory for me too.

'I'll miss you, Jimmy,' I said quietly, wiping the tears away with my forearms, as I walked away, retracing my steps back through the graveyard.

'Cheerio, love,' called the old man, raising his arm to me.

'Bye and thanks,' I managed to say through the tears as I fumbled in my pockets to find a tissue.

Less than ten minutes later, I'd made my way to the

village centre and was standing outside Honeysuckle Cottage, admiring the picture-postcard effect of the vines climbing the oak porch and the hanging baskets, already in bloom, framing the doorway. It was prettier than I could ever have imagined. Before I'd had time to consider what I was doing, I rapped on the door-knocker three times, half hoping that no one would be in so that I could drift away, as if I'd never been there, and climb back in the car and make my way home.

No such luck. The door eased open and Jimmy's mum Rosemary greeted me, looking tanned and relaxed in a short-sleeved checked blouse and cream chinos, her hands covered by floral gardening gloves. She looked as if she didn't have a care in the world. What was I doing here, stirring up who knew what?

'Hello!'

'Hello, Rosemary, you won't remember me, but...'

'Of course I remember you,' she said, standing back and pulling the door open further, her face lighting up. 'It's Alice, isn't it? How lovely to see you. Do come in. You'll have to excuse me,' she added, brushing herself down, 'I was just in the garden, doing some pruning.'

'Thanks. I hope I'm not intruding, though.' I wandered after Rosemary down the narrow hallway, looking first one way and then the other, my gaze distracted by the photos on the wall as Jimmy's eyes stared down at me from all angles.

'No, not at all. I'm grateful for the break. Come on through into the kitchen. I was just thinking it must be time for a cup of tea.'

The old-fashioned country kitchen was full of French oak cabinets brimming with brightly coloured crockery. A vase of cream tulips sat in the middle of the huge rectory table, complementing the deep ochre of the walls. An image of Jimmy pulling out a chair and sitting down at the table, something he must have done a million times before, flashed into my mind.

'Have a seat,' Rosemary said, bringing me back to the present. She filled the kettle from the tap, placing it in its holder, before turning to face me. 'So how are you?' she asked.

'I'm very well. I was just passing,' I fibbed, 'and

it was such a lovely afternoon, I decided to come and visit Jimmy's grave.'

'Oh, well, I'm very glad you did. It's such a beautiful spot, isn't it? I find it a great comfort knowing he's there, not five minutes around the corner. I often wander down there of an evening and spend some time with him.'

My gaze drifted out of the leaded window and into the garden. Now I was here, sitting in Jimmy's family home, I wasn't sure what it was I'd come for. There was so much I wanted to tell Rosemary; that she wasn't to worry, that Jimmy was happy, that he was doing a good job of making himself very comfortable in my home, that he was eating his way through the contents of my cupboards, but I couldn't tell her any of that. Instead, I helped myself to a chocolate digestive from the plate Rosemary offered once she'd joined me at the table with our tea.

'It is lovely, so peaceful,' I agreed. 'And how have you both been keeping?' I asked, observing her reaction thoughtfully.

She sighed, placing her mug of tea back on the table.

'Well, of course, it's been hard. The mornings are the worst. Waking up and thinking for a moment that things are just the same as they ever were. Then comes the awful realisation,' she slapped her hands together hard, her eyes, the same greyish hue as Jimmy's, brimming with emotion, 'and it's like reliving that awful moment over again, when we were first told the news, knowing that life will never be the same again.' Her shoulders sagged as she locked her fingers together and rested her chin on her hands. 'Michael copes by keeping busy. He barely sits still. He's out now,' she explained. 'He drives the local community bus, taking the old folk into town.' She smiled wryly. 'Me, I'm happy pottering at home. It gives me a sense of comfort being in the place where we spent so many happy times together.'

'I can understand that.'

'Of course, it helps knowing that he was loved by so many people. You wouldn't believe the numbers of letters and cards we've received through the post. Here, let me show you.' She pulled out a wicker basket that had been sitting on one of the kitchen chairs tucked beneath the table, picked up a pile of letters, and allowed them to drop back into the basket. 'It's been very humbling. I'm slowing working my way through the heap, but I'm determined to reply to them all.'

I ran my hands through the stack of letters and cards, shaking my head in disbelief. 'Jimmy would be overwhelmed by the reaction, don't you think?'

Her laughter tinkled around the room, a room I was certain had heard a great deal of laughter over the years.

'Oh, yes, he would have loved all the fuss and adulation. He was just like that as a little boy, you know. Attention seeking! Playing up to the crowd. Acting the joker. Charming his audience. To think he's still doing it after his death, well, it makes me smile.'

If only you knew, I thought, smiling at her fondly.

'Ryan was absolutely right. James was a golden boy. Everything he tried his hand at he turned into a success. He expected it as his given, really, I suppose we all did. We all thought he was at the beginning of what would have been a long and fruitful phase at the top of his game, career-wise. The happy personal life, a wife, children, a beautiful home, were surely just around the corner for him.'

She shrugged wistfully.

'The strange thing is,' she went on, 'although it's been hard, very hard, since we lost Jimmy, I've been strangely comforted by his presence in these difficult weeks.' She shrugged her shoulders, laying her hands open on the table, as if she didn't quite believe it herself. 'I'd heard people say before that they'd felt the presence of their loved ones around them when they'd passed and I'd never really believed it, but now, well, I've experienced it for myself.'

'Really?' was all I could manage to say.

'Oh, yes. Sometimes I feel as if he's here, looking over us, making sure we're okay. You probably think me mad, but Michael says he feels it too, and he's a proper sceptic.'

I'd been a sceptic too until I'd had my very own first-hand experience of living alongside a ghost.

'I don't think you're mad at all.' I ran my finger along a groove in the tabletop. 'I think there's so much we don't know about the whole dying process and what happens on the other side. It's reassuring to think that there might be something else out there, after all.'

Rosemary nodded and we sat in companionable silence for a few moments until she looked across at me, her eyes smiling mischievously.

'Now, tell me to mind my own business, but what I'd like to know is what sort of relationship you had with Jimmy? I suspect it was something more than just a friendship. Am I wrong?' She raised her eyebrows, tilting her head to one side, a smile resting on her lips.

Anything I told her would be an untruth, so all I could do was tell her my own version of the truth that existed in my own skew-whiff world.

'We are...' I stopped myself. 'We were very close. I hadn't known Jimmy long, but we became good friends in a short space of time, and I suppose I feel cheated that we weren't able to get to know each other better. Who knows, we might have quickly grown to hate each other, but I don't think so. We seemed to click instantly, like you do with some people. I'd like to think we would have played a constant role, one way or the other, in each other's lives.'

With her friendly face cupped in her hands, observing me thoughtfully, opening up to Rosemary felt easy and entirely natural. To talk to someone who knew Jimmy even more intimately than I did was poignant and therapeutic at the same time and I could tell from her warm expression that she felt exactly the same way. 'One thing I do know,' I continued, 'is that he was the loveliest, most decent man I'd met in a very long while.'

'I knew it,' Rosemary said with a touch of triumph. 'I said to Michael when we met you at the funeral that I thought you were someone special in Jimmy's life. It was just a feeling I had. Jimmy had reached that stage in his life where he was ready to meet someone special, to settle down and start a family.' Her eyes took on a misty faraway look. 'He would have made a lovely father.' She paused, took a deep breath and looked me directly in the eye. 'I suppose you're as distraught as we are about the stories in the press?'

My stomach tensed.

'You mean Donna Diamond, I suppose?'

'Yes... we... I mean...' She faltered, her voice tight with emotion.

'That was something I wanted to talk to you about,' I said, suddenly feeling uncertain. I took hold of her hand across the table, wondering how she might react to the next bombshell I was about to drop. 'This is very difficult,' I started.

'Go on,' she said. She smiled wryly. 'Whatever it is can be no worse than what we've already had to endure.'

'There's no easy way to say this, but what you've read in the papers, about the baby. I'm afraid it simply isn't true. It isn't Jimmy's baby, Rosemary.'

'I knew it!' She banged her hand down on the table. 'I just knew it.' She sat back in her chair, the pain evident in the soft lines of her face. 'But how can you possibly know this?' she added, quietly.

'I know Donna. I've spoken to her, and she's admitted the baby isn't Jimmy's. She never even had any kind of relationship with him. It was just a lie, I'm afraid. Something she made up on the spur of the moment, a chance to cash in on Jimmy's name, I suppose, not realising that it would escalate into such a big deal.'

Rosemary shook her head, all her energy seeming to drain from her body.

'But why would she do that? It's an awful thing to do. Really awful. It was so out of character for Jimmy, though, so far away from the person that he was, that we knew it couldn't possibly be true.' She pulled out a tissue from the box on the other end of the table and dabbed at her eyes. 'But to think that there would be a part of Jimmy, his baby, growing up in the world, we couldn't help imagining what that might be like.'

'I know, I know,' I said, feeling desperately sad for her. To lose at first her son and then the possibility of a future grandchild, it was almost too much to bear. I stood up and walked around to her side, wrapping my arms around her. 'I'm so sorry, Rosemary. Really, I am.'

'It's for the best,' she said, through her tears, as she collapsed into my arms, her shoulders juddering. My tears came then too, and as we held each other, taking comfort from one another, I knew then, despite my reservations, it had been exactly the right thing to do coming here today.

'Everything okay?'

We pulled away from each other and turned to see Michael standing in the doorway, a bemused expression on his face. I gasped. It could have been Jimmy standing there, the likeness was so pronounced; the same laughing deep-set eyes, the same jawline, but it was the rich warm tone to the voice that sent shivers running down my spine.

'Darling! You remember Alice, don't you?'

'Of course I do,' said Michael, his face lighting up, as welcoming and friendly as his wife. 'How lovely to see you, Alice.'

'You're just in time. We were just about to have a glass of wine, weren't we, Alice?' She patted me on the hand, and I knew I'd found myself a friend for life. 'Would you do the honours, dear?' she said to Michael fondly. 'I'll go and fetch the albums and show Alice some pictures of Jimmy when he was a boy.'

22

By the time I got back to the flat, it was after ten, and I wasn't expecting Jimmy to be home as he'd gone off on a little jaunt over to France to catch up with someone he'd been at school with. So I was a little bit surprised to find the front door to my flat wide open.

'Jimmy?' I called as I wandered in.

I heard furtive movements from the kitchen and my heart lifted at the thought of Jimmy being home early, preparing my dinner. I had so much to tell him.

'Hi, I didn't expect to find...' I stopped mid-sentence in the doorway to the kitchen as a young man dressed in jeans and a grey hoodie delved into my coffee jar. He turned and looked at me darkly.

'Shit!' he said, dropping the top to the coffee jar on the floor and dashing past me, almost pushing me out of the way.

'Hey,' I said, 'don't rush off. You're a friend of Jimmy's, aren't you?' With his pasty complexion and deep black circles beneath his eyes, he was clearly not of this world.

'Eh?' he said, turning to look at me.

A frisson of fear shivered down my body. Oh, please, Lord, not another one! What if I was expected to look after this motley-looking ghoul as well as Jimmy? Or perhaps this new creature was a replacement for Jimmy, and this was now my designated role in life; looking after one wayward spirit after another.

At least Jimmy had the benefit of being easy on the eye, was delightfully charming with his outrageous yet entertaining stories and could rustle up a mean cheese omelette at the drop of a hat. The guy in front of me couldn't even look me in the eye, had seemingly lost the capacity for coherent speech and what, exactly, was that awful smell? My nostrils twitched at the scent of something really nasty.

Still, if I'd been granted the special power by an unknown higher mystical authority to act as a go-between for the newly dead before they were moved on to wherever it was they were off to, then I really shouldn't abuse my position by not at least pretending to be friendly.

'I expect you're hungry. Would you like something to eat?' I asked brightly, remembering when Jimmy first turned up he was absolutely ravenous and spent the first three days emptying my cupboards of all my food.

'What? Are you having a laugh?'

Clearly this particular spook hadn't been to the same charm school as Jimmy.

'Well, how about a bath, then? Let's get you out of those grubby clothes. You'll feel so much better after a long deep soak.'

'What the...?'

'Look, I know this situation is all very strange, but I promise you, you'll get used to it. I found it strange too when I first came across Jimmy because he was the first, um... one of your kind that I'd ever met.'

'One of my kind?'

'Yes, you can imagine how it freaked me out,' I laughed, hoping it might bring a smile to his grouchy face. 'Jimmy was...'

'And who the fuck is Jimmy? Leave it out, love. I know your type. Trying to be friendly and all that bollocks. What are you? Some kind of do-gooder or something?'

Obviously this pitiful creature was having trouble adjusting to his new-found position in the stratosphere and would need much gentler handling than Jimmy in accepting his new reality.

'Cut the crap, love, and just hand over the money.' His lip curled menacingly, as he pushed his face up close to mine.

'The... money?' I faltered. 'What money? What do you mean?' His face glowered darker and an uneasy feeling swept through my body as the dawning realisation hit me. 'I get it! You're... you're not a... ghost, are you? You're... oh, my goodness... you're a... *thief!*' A high-pitched scream reverberated off the walls. Startled, I looked around to make sure it wasn't someone else making the awful noise. No, it was definitely all of my own making.

'Hang on a minute,' said the youth, looking genuinely puzzled. 'Did you just call me a ghost?'

'Ha, forget it,' I laughed brightly, trying to appear as if I was really quite normal, but after our earlier exchange, I think I'd completely blown that pretence.

'No, you forget it, I'm out of here,' he said, turning on his heel and running towards the door. 'You're not right in the head, do you know that?'

He snatched up my handbag from the hallway and legged it outside, running straight into Jimmy's frankly overdue presence as he sauntered in through the front door.

'Jesus Christ!' cried the youth as he was spun around on the spot, dropping the bag and its contents all over the floor. 'What the hell was that?' He looked over his shoulder at me, his eyes wide with fear, and shook his head.

Jimmy, noticing my stricken expression, rushed towards me as I heard the lad's footsteps pound down the stairs. I fell into Jimmy's arms, my whole body shaking uncontrollably.

'It's okay, it's okay,' he said, patting my back, his breath soothing against my cheek. 'Everything's okay, you're safe now. I'm home.'

* * *

After two mugs of sweetened tea and some pacing up and down, reliving each moment of my terrifying encounter, the shaking gradually subsided, and I began to feel a tiny bit better.

'Do you think I should call the police?' I asked Jimmy as I hugged my arms around my chest.

'If you think it will make you feel better, but to be honest, judging by that guy's horrified face when I relieved him of your property, I don't think you'll be seeing him around here again.' He put his arm around my shoulder, squeezing it gently. 'He was probably just a druggie, chancing his arm. Might be worth you getting the lock on the front door changed, though, just to be on the safe side.' He smiled and ruffled my hair. 'Have you calmed down a bit now?' he asked.

'Just about, I think.' I paused, turning to look at him. 'It was such a shock, that was all. To think that a complete stranger invaded my home and was helping himself to my things. I couldn't believe it. It was only afterwards I realised the danger I was in. He could have attacked me, murdered me, even!'

Jimmy raised his eyebrows, nodding his head sagely.

'He could have done!' I protested, noting his doubtful expression. 'And where the hell were you, exactly?' I chided, immediately regretting the words.

'Well, not there, certainly.' A wry smile rested on his lips. 'Not yet, at least.'

His words brought me up short.

'Stop it. You know what I mean. You left it a bit late coming to my rescue.'

'Yeah, sorry about that. But I got here, didn't I? Just in the nick of time, I'd say.'

'I suppose,' I said chastising him with a look. I had no right to feel upset or let down, but I'd been so used to Jimmy turning up instantly whenever there was a problem that I couldn't help feeling a bit huffy. I sighed. 'What are you laughing at?' I said crossly, noticing his amused expression.

'Well, you have to admit it's funny. All the time

you thought the guy was a ghost, you were quite happy having him in the flat, even offering him dinner. It was only when you found out he wasn't one of the living dead, but that he was actually a living person, admittedly a thief, that you freaked out.'

'I'm glad you find it so amusing,' I said, elbowing him in the ribs and joining in reluctantly with the laughter. 'It just goes to show what a mess my life is in at the moment. I can't make sense of anything these days. Do you think I'll ever get back to any kind of normality? I'm not even sure I know what normal is now.'

'I'm sorry.' Jimmy's brow creased, his dark eyes observing me thoughtfully. 'I've really screwed things up for you, haven't I?'

'No, of course you haven't. I didn't mean it like that. Come here,' I said, my arms finding his waist and drawing him close. His body next to mine felt so very real; strong, hard and dependable. Not like I'd expect a ghost to feel at all. In my embrace, Jimmy felt all man. My head rested against his chest. I could even imagine I heard his heart beating. 'I wouldn't change any part of this weird and wonderful experience. It's been... amazing. Strange, but amazing. And apart from all the weird stuff, I've really liked having you around. I always thought I was happy living alone, pleasing no one but myself, but this, you being here, has been so much better, a real eye-opener.'

'Yeah, it's been great,' he said, a wistful note to his voice.

I gazed up into his face and I wasn't sure if I imagined the look of longing in his eyes or whether that was just wishful thinking on my part. When I felt his lips land gently on mine, our mouths parting at the same moment, I knew for certain what his eyes had been telling me.

'I just wish it didn't have to be like this.' He sighed, pulling away before tracing a finger along my jawline, his feather-light touch sending a surge of desire through my body.

'No, me neither,' I said breathlessly, looking into his eyes, wanting so much more, yet knowing it was futile; there was nothing he could offer me.

'Hey, you haven't forgotten about Friday, have you?' He dropped his hands to his sides and turned away, walking off into the kitchen. I heard him running a glass of water from the tap.

My head spun, a whirl of thoughts fighting for attention as his tender touch lingered on my lips.

'Friday?'

'Yeah, you know, we talked about having a day out together. The forecast's good, we could go down by the river, take a picnic.'

I ran my hands through my hair, shaking my head, my whole body still a quivering mess from Jimmy's kiss.

'Oh, Jimmy, I'd love to, but I can't just take a day off work at such short notice. You know that.' I gladly relieved him of the glass of water he was holding and took a large slug.

'You've got the day off, don't you remember? Really, Alice, I don't know what's got into you these last few weeks, but your memory is truly shocking. Have a look in the diary tomorrow when you get into work, you'll see for yourself, you've got a day's holiday booked.'

'Jimmy, you didn't, did you? How could you... when...'

'Well,' he shrugged, looking sheepish, 'I only had your emotional wellbeing in mind. You deserve a day's rest, some pampering, and your boss is off at the moment, so what's there to stop you?'

I laughed, shaking my head in exasperation.

'You're outrageous, Jimmy, completely outrageous. Do you know that?'

* * *

'Right,' said Damon, removing the battery from his drill and placing it back in its box. 'That's the new lock sorted.' He opened and shut my front door by way of demonstration. 'Let someone try and force their way through that now.' He stood back, admiring his handiwork. 'You'll be able to sleep safe in your bed tonight.'

'Thanks, Damon,' I sighed, feeling properly relieved and handing him a mug of tea for all his effort. He'd rung earlier to arrange a meeting for lunch to discuss his business set-up, as we'd planned, but no sooner had I mentioned the break-in than he'd insisted on coming round to check that the door and windows were completely secure. 'I really appreciate all the trouble you've gone to.'

'It's no trouble,' he said. 'I didn't like the thought of you feeling vulnerable in your own home.'

'Well, not now I won't.' Certainly not with two eligible men looking after my emotional and physical wellbeing, I wouldn't. Although, I supposed only one of the men could be considered as eligible. Being part of the walking dead, even if you were still extremely hot, precluded you from making it to the top of the 100 Most Eligible Bachelors list.

I'd hoped Jimmy would have made himself scarce, but he'd been hanging around ever since Damon arrived, making a nuisance of himself and a string of disparaging remarks too.

'Ah, well, I see Bob the Builder has come to your rescue, so I'll leave you in his capable hands. I wouldn't want to get in the way.' Jimmy blew me a kiss from across the room and even at a distance he could still send shivers down my spine.

'Are you all right?' Damon asked, looking concerned, as he caught me shuddering.

'Oh, yes, fine. Someone just walked over my grave, that's all.' My voice rang out unnaturally high.

'Probably the shock of all this nasty business.'

'Hmmm,' I said, nodding furiously, hoping Jimmy would take the hint and leave, sooner rather than later.

'Ooh-er, dinky little toolbox he has there,' Jimmy added, puckering his lips and winking at me in that cheeky way of his as he bent down to look at Damon's gear scattered on the floor.

'I'll just fetch my tea and come and sit down with you,' I told Damon.

Out of sight, I gave Jimmy the benefit of one of my looks, one I'd become practised at ever since he'd turned up in my life, and hissed at him.

'Stop it. He'll wonder what's going on. Why don't you go now and stop being a pain?' It had been all I could do to stop myself from giggling at Jimmy's antics. 'Damon's been very kind. I don't want to offend him.'

'No, of course you don't. He's a proper all-round action man, isn't he?' he said, none too sincerely.

He wafted down the hallway and out through the front door, reappearing seconds later with a mischievous glint in his eye.

'Now you see me,' he said waving his arms in

the air, 'now you don't.' The vanishing act was funny, even though I'd seen it a hundred times before. 'Hmm, maybe Mr Action Man's high-tech security installation isn't quite as safe as he'd like to think. What a shame. You might still be vulnerable to some spooky late-night visitations from your very favourite ghoul. Sorry about that!'

'Jimmy, just go, would you?' I said, through the side of mouth, trying and failing to be cross at him.

'I'm on my way. See you later, gorgeous. Love you.' And he was gone, his words echoing loudly in my head.

Love you? Had I heard him right? No, he'd definitely used those two little words.

Not *the* three little words, but two. And I wondered if the missing word made all the difference. Despite my galloping heartbeat and the flush of heat creeping up my neck, I told myself it was just a throwaway remark. Nothing more. The sort of thing you'd say to a very good friend. Which is what we were. Good friends.

Although I'd known for some time now that it was so much more than that for me. I loved him. Three little words. In every conceivable way.

23

'This is the life!' Arms above my head, reclining in the warmth of the late spring afternoon with the sun upon my face, I gazed up, in awe of Jimmy's mastery as he navigated the punt along the still waters of the River Cherwell.

'People alert,' he said grinning and I jumped up, squeezing in the space between him and the pole, attempting to look as though I knew what I was supposed to be doing while Jimmy did all the hard work behind me. I gave a cheery wave to the onlookers who were clearly admiring my effortless boating skills as our punt made its way smoothly on its path.

'It's glorious, isn't it?' he said, when we'd passed by, taking control again, and I'd resumed my reclining, savouring-the-moment position. 'This is something I've always wanted to do. Messing about on the river.'

'Lovely,' I agreed, laughing, 'especially as I'm not having to do any of the hard work.'

I let my fingertips dangle in the cool water as Jimmy guided the boat to a spot on the far side of the river and came and sat down with me.

'What would Madame like for lunch?' he asked, opening the wicker hamper he'd stuffed full to the brim with goodies. 'How about a glass of champagne to start?'

'Wow, I wasn't expecting all this.' My eyes grew large at the feast of tempting goodies laid bare. Olives, smoked salmon bites, cheese straws and strawberries.

'I lied about the glass,' he said, his eyes twinkling, as he handed me a drink, 'but a plastic flute is the next best thing.'

'I could get used to this.' I grinned. The gentle breeze lifted my hair and as I sipped on my champagne, its honeyed undertones tinged on my tongue, delightfully complementing the sweetness of the juicy strawberries. It was easy to imagine I'd died and gone to heaven. After all, I had my very own guardian angel watching over me, a wry smile upon his face.

'Well, I thought it was about time I treated you after everything you've done for me. You've been a real star, Alice.' He unwrapped a foil package and revealed a stack of egg and cress sandwiches. 'When I think of the places I could have ended up, it makes me shudder. Just imagine being landed in a house with stroppy teenagers or a couple of screaming babies or, worse still, student digs, all those dirty dishes and smelly socks, or even sharing a cardboard box with a tramp!'

Jimmy was partial to his creature comforts. I couldn't imagine him slumming it.

'No, I definitely picked the long straw when I was delivered into the very capable hands of a single, gorgeous, extremely eligible young woman.'

I smiled, running my tongue across my lips, basking in Jimmy's flattery.

'Of course, I don't think there was anything random about my placement with you.'

'You don't?' I asked, looking at him warily.

'No, why, do you?' he asked directly, catching me unawares. I shrugged, keeping quiet as he went on. 'There's obviously a reason why I was foisted upon you and not into the care of a bunch of students or an old tramp.'

'And, um, what do you think that reason might be?'

'Unfinished business, I suppose.'

'Yeah, that business with Donna. I suppose now it's all been cleared up, you'll be moved over.' It tore at my heart even to think about it. 'Maybe they're just waiting for the article to appear in the magazine first.'

Jimmy laughed.

'I was wrong about that.'

'Sorry?'

'Thinking that was the reason for me being stuck here. I mean, I'm glad I got the opportunity to sort all that out, but that wasn't the reason I hadn't moved over.'

'It wasn't?'

'No. And I don't know why it didn't occur to me

before. I mean, it's been staring us in the face from the very first moment we met.'

'It has?' I said, my voice squeaky.

'Yes, I think we both know that you and I were due to meet in real life and because of what happened,' he shrugged, laughing, 'my unexpected demise and all that, it never came to anything. This is a second chance, I suppose. An opportunity to tie up some ends, find some resolution.'

'And do you think you've done that now?'

'Well, not as extensively as I would have liked to, obviously, but at least I got to meet you at last, to spend some time with you.' He smiled, his dark eyes looking up at me from beneath long lashes. 'That's what all this has been about. Finding you. We were meant to be together, you and me, you know that?' He reached out for my hand, our fingers interlocking.

Hearing the words from Jimmy's lips sent short sharp stabbing pains around my body, my breath quickening until I thought my heart might burst. My hands felt clammy as I gripped onto the side of the boat. I couldn't bring myself to meet Jimmy's gaze.

'Funny you should say that,' I said examining the bottom slats of the boat, trying to keep my tone light, 'because Lexie said exactly the same thing.'

'Really? She's a bright girl, your sister. A pain in the arse at times, but a very bright girl.'

The look we exchanged and our shared ripple of laughter broke the sizzling tension as he squeezed my hand tighter.

'I know. She showed me that clip on YouTube, the interview you gave to Margot.'

Jimmy nodded. 'We filmed that the week before I died. It was the first time I'd spoken publicly about my personal life.'

'It was really touching.'

'I meant every word of it.' There was a sincerity underlining his words, as his gaze, fixed firmly upon my eyes, burrowed deep into my soul. 'I'd been waiting a lifetime to meet you, Alice, and, on borrowed time, on my way out the back door, I finally managed to do it. I guess my timing wasn't brilliant.'

Tears swelled in my eyes and the fine hairs on my arms stood on end at the realisation of the painful futility of our situation. There would be no happy ending written in the stars for us. Where Jimmy was going, it was a single one-way trip only. And my name wasn't even on the passenger ticket. Certainly not for this particular departure.

I examined my fingernails, pushing back my cuticles with my thumb.

'Who knows, it might not have worked out for us. I guess we'll never know for sure.'

Jimmy raised an eyebrow, giving a wry smile.

'I know,' he said, sadly. 'There's not many things I'm certain about these days, but I know this much. We would have been very happy together, Alice. Forever and ever and all that.' He shrugged, smiling, but I couldn't help noticing the pain flickering in his deep grey eyes. 'We clicked from the start, you and me, just as we would have done if we'd been lucky enough to meet in real life when I could have actually done something about it.' He took a deep breath before exhaling slowly.

'Alice Fletcher,' he said, leaning over and picking up my hand, 'I love you. With all my heart. And I want you to know that I always will. I can go to my resting place, wherever and whenever that might be, knowing that this here,' he tapped his chest, 'is filled with my love for you.'

My heart soared as a surge of red-hot emotion ran riot through my body, filling every aching pore.

'I love you too, Jimmy Mack,' I admitted, as the tears that had been pricking at my eyes ran freely down my cheeks. 'But this is so unfair! We've only just found each other and now we'll be torn apart. Why, Jimmy? It just doesn't make sense.'

'I don't know,' he said, his shoulders slumping in defeat. 'I don't have the answer to that one. But we can't afford to think like that, Alice. We have to be grateful that we finally found each other, even if it is a bit late. The thought of leaving you behind breaks my heart. I don't want to lose you, Alice, not now I've only just found you, but however much it saddens me, you still have your whole life left to live here, without me. This is how it has to be.'

I looked into his eyes, seeing the emotion brimming within.

'What I do know is that you'll always have my heart,' he said, thumping his chest with his fist. 'Some people go a whole lifetime never meeting that someone special. I nearly missed out on it myself, so I know how lucky I am. I just hope you'll hang onto a small part of my heart as well.'

'Believe me, I will!' I cried, the tears now giving way to huge gulping sobs. 'But I don't know how I'll ever survive without you.'

'You have to, Alice. There is no alternative.' The steeliness of his voice made my heart turn cold. 'This is what we've been handed and we have to get on with it. Make the most of the time we do have together, make every second count.'

He got up on his haunches and leant over towards me, his lips finding mine. The boat rocked precariously and I laughed away my tears as he steadied himself on the side. His kiss was tender, sensual and urgent all at the same time, the pent-up tension held in my arms and legs melting away in an instant under his gentle caress. Locked together in an embrace, we fell backwards onto the hard wooden slats of the boat, oblivious to anything or anyone, lost in the delicious exploration of each other's bodies.

As all my inhibitions were diving overboard and I was ready to sink into the depths of blissful oblivion, from nowhere a tremendous crash juddered our little boat, causing us to list dramatically. I fell over to one side and grabbed the edge, water splashing up the side of the boat spraying my face, my heart thumping as I looked to Jimmy for reassurance.

'What on earth are you doing, you stupid woman?'

I looked up, peering over the side of the boat, to see a tall man in a striped blazer, a straw boater and an irate expression hanging onto the pole of his vessel as if he might catapult himself over and join me on mine.

'I'm sorry,' I spluttered, crawling on to my knees and waving my arms from side to side in an attempt to regain some balance. 'I was, um, just enjoying the sunshine, such a lovely day, isn't it? I didn't re-alise I was drifting, I must have nodded off,' I said woefully, noticing we were a long way from where we'd moored. I adjusted my clothing, hoping he wouldn't notice the pink flush of desire that had covered my arms and neck.

Jimmy reached for the paddle, laughing, and attempted to manoeuvre us out of the way of the other boat.

'There is such a thing as river etiquette, you know,' the man said huffily. He pushed his pole against our boat and veered away from us. 'We'd all like to lounge around without giving a care or thought to anyone else on the river, but there are rules to obey, you know?'

'Plonker,' said Jimmy, dipping his oar deep in the river and flicking it in the direction of the man, drenching him from head to toe.

'Good grief, what was that?' He looked at me accusingly.

'A fish,' I said, excitedly. 'This big, it was.' I held my hands out wide by way of explanation. 'A trout, I think,' I said, conjuring up the first fish that came to mind.

'Don't be ridiculous,' said the man, wiping himself down. 'There aren't any trout in this stretch of water.'

'A big brown fish, then. Like a trout. But not a trout, obviously. Sorry. I'm very sorry,' I grovelled, trying to ignore the small crowd of amused onlookers who'd gathered by the riverbank. I reacquainted myself with the pole and hung onto it for dear life, beckoning Jimmy with a desperate wide-eyed look to help me.

'Let me,' he said, laughing, coming to my rescue and taking the pole out of my hands. 'Let's get you out of here before you get yourself into any more trouble.' He steered us towards the mooring. 'Come on, I need to get you home so we can finish what we started here before we were so rudely interrupted.'

He winked at me, and my stomach went into freefall.

24

'Are you okay, Alice? You seem a bit distracted, that's all. We could always do this some other time, if you'd prefer?'

'Oh, I'm sorry, Damon,' I said, dragging my attention back from where it had flitted out of the window. I looked across the table of the very exclusive restaurant he'd brought me to, his face now a picture of concern. A quick coffee and a bite to eat in the local café was what I'd been expecting, but this felt far too much like a date for my liking and that was the last thing I wanted. I didn't want to be here, alone with Damon. I wanted to be back at my flat with Jimmy.

I'd barely touched my food and had felt listless and detached all evening. It wasn't Damon's fault that I was such terrible company.

'I've been a bit preoccupied lately,' I offered by way of explanation for my unscintillating company. 'Family problems, you know how it is.'

Damon nodded sympathetically.

He must have thought I had the most dysfunctional family since the Munsters, the number of times I'd brought them and their myriad of problems up these last few weeks.

'But your business, I've jotted down a few ideas here for some systems you might want to consider implementing. If you like, I can come in for a day or two to your office and we can make a start on setting up your accounts and admin procedures, if you think that might help.'

'That would be great. But I would hate to impose while you have so many other things on your plate.' He picked up my hastily scribbled notes, running his finger down the page. 'I'm sure this will give me plenty to work on for the time being.'

He smiled, putting the papers to one side, and I couldn't help feeling guilty that it must have been perfectly apparent my heart wasn't in this whole thing.

The trouble was, since that gloriously special day I'd spent with Jimmy on the river, I hadn't been able to think of anything else, replaying every single moment over and over in my mind. It had been a bittersweet day with lots of outpourings of emotions, some tears from us both, but mostly a great deal of laughter. But it had brought home to me just how much Jimmy had come to mean to me and how much I would inevitably have to lose.

Being here with Damon in the sophisticated surroundings of the exclusive country club with its sweeping lawns and classical statues only reinforced everything I would never be able to share with Jimmy.

Jimmy and I could never be a proper couple. We'd never be able to go out together to a swanky restaurant like this. Nor would I be able to introduce him to my friends and family. We wouldn't be able to go on holiday together. Or buy a house or get engaged or have a huge over-the-top wedding with too many guests or make lots of beautiful babies together.

It was all futile fantasy, and yet my every waking moment was spent tormenting myself with what-might-have-beens and what-could-have-beens, Jimmy's words playing on a loop in my head.

'We have no future together, darling. All we have is the here and now for as long as it may last. But you can't put your life on hold for me. Take it from me, I should know, you need to live for the moment, as you never know what might be round the corner.'

But that was impossible. All the time Jimmy was around, he had to be the most important priority in my life. After all, I was the only person he had in this strange halfway world he inhabited. But more than that, I loved him. With all my heart. I was trapped by the situation just as much as Jimmy was.

How I wished I could open up to Damon and tell him exactly what was going on in my life and the size of the insurmountable problem I'd been landed with. He was a strategist, one of life's big thinkers. If anyone could come up with a solution to my problem, it would be Damon. But I simply couldn't. I couldn't talk to anyone other than Lexie about my situation and that left me living in that same twilight world as Jimmy.

I looked across at Damon, feeling a painful mix of regret and disappointment. He was such a lovely guy; he didn't deserve to be landed with a mixed-up girl like me who kept company with the strangest of folk.

'I'm really sorry, Damon, but I should go now.' I felt the tears rush to my eyes and I turned away, blinking them back. I shouldn't have been sitting here with Damon when I could have been at home with Jimmy, spending what precious time we had left together. Who knew, it was probably only going to be a matter of weeks or days as it was. Claustrophobia threatened to overwhelm me as my throat tightened and I struggled to find my breath. I needed to get out of here, away from the bewilderment in Damon's eyes and back to Jimmy where I belonged. I stood up and made a dash for the main entrance.

'Hey, it's okay, Alice, I'll take you home,' Damon said kindly.

'No, there's no need, I can make my own way. I'll

grab a taxi or something. It's all right. You stay, finish your meal.'

Panic washed over me, an overwhelming urgency filling every pore of my body, telling me I needed to get back home as quickly as possible.

'It's okay,' said Damon, a voice of reason in an increasingly suffocating atmosphere. He stood up, settled the bill and ushered me outside towards the car.

I sank down into the passenger seat, looking forlornly out of the window, unable to find any words that might offer Damon the explanation he deserved.

By the time we drew up in front of my block, the air between us was tight with an awkward silence.

'Thanks, Damon, for a lovely evening. I mean it.' My voice sounded unnatural even to me.

His eyes met mine for the briefest of moments but long enough for me to notice the hurt and disappointment within.

I pushed open the car door, almost falling out, and ran up to the front door. Looking round, I waved to Damon, but his gaze was fixed firmly ahead. Dejectedly, I shoved open the double doors, feeling like a total bitch, and once inside, I heard the car rev up and pull away.

I fumbled with the keys, finally falling through the front door.

'Hey, you,' Jimmy called, 'did you have a good time?'

Relief washed over me. He was still here. Where he should be. I ran through into the living room.

'You're still here?' I said, just to make sure my tired eyes weren't deceiving me.

'Yes, Alice, I'm still here. I made you a promise, don't you remember?'

'I know, but every time I go out, I worry that when I come back, you'll be gone. It's a horrible feeling, Jimmy, really horrible.' I bit on my lip to stop the tears from falling.

'I know.' He nodded, his face full of kindness and understanding. 'Come here and give me a hug. You look shattered.'

He wrapped his arms around me and ran his hand through my hair. My body felt so weary, I thought I might collapse into his embrace.

'You need to go to bed. It's been a tough couple of days. Go on,' he said kissing me lightly on the lips, sending me on my way. 'Jump straight into bed. I'll see you in the morning.'

'Sleep tight, Jimmy.'

'You too, Alice.'

In the bedroom, I hurriedly stepped out of my dress and threw it on the wicker chair in the corner before flinging myself on the bed where I sobbed myself, very quietly, to sleep.

25

'Are you ready for a cuppa?' Jimmy asked tentatively, his smiling face peering around the bedroom door. I groaned and pulled the duvet further up over my head.

The sun was being annoyingly chirpy for such an early hour, filtering through the cream linen curtains, insisting that it was time to wake up, but the only thing I was interested in was the deepest darkest recesses of my bed. I tried lifting my head to meet the day, but it only throbbed in protest.

'Let me draw the curtains, let a bit of daylight in. It's a beautiful morning out there.'

I was sure it was, but I didn't want any part of it.

Maybe if I just snuggled under the covers and slept for a very long time, everything would be okay by the time I woke up.

'There you go,' said Jimmy, placing the mug on the bedside table. Such a simple thing, but it always brightened my day. It was a habit he'd got into from the very first day he'd turned up in my flat, bringing me my early morning mug of tea, one I was quite happy for him to continue with for as long as he intended hanging around. Who would do that for me once he was gone? I thought with a pang. Now, though, he leant over me, those deep soulful grey eyes examining me intently.

'Good grief,' he said, running a finger down my cheek, 'you look dreadful. You haven't got food poisoning, have you?'

'Uggh.' I sank further back into my pillows. 'No, I haven't got food poisoning. Thank you for your concern.'

'Uh-oh. Have you been crying, then? That's it, isn't it? What happened? Not that bastard, Damon? I thought he was too good to be true. Jesus.' He shook his head, his lips held tight together in anger. 'I knew I should have kept an eye on you.'

I put my hand up to my head, to shield the light, trying to stop the sharp needle jabbing at my forehead. 'No, no, it was nothing like that. It was a lovely evening, but it just felt so awkward, so difficult. I couldn't enjoy myself, thinking of you being stuck here alone, and I didn't pay any attention to Damon. He must have thought me really rude.'

Jimmy positioned himself next to me on the bed, plumping up the cushions, before leaning back on the headboard. He handed me a box of tissues and I pulled one out, blowing my nose noisily. I could cry at the drop of a hat these days.

'I'm cramping your style, aren't I? You shouldn't have to worry about me when you're out trying to enjoy yourself. It's not fair. Far too much to expect of you.'

'That's exactly it,' I said, throwing a pillow randomly across the room. 'I can never get away from you and this awful situation we've found ourselves in.'

His forlorn expression bore down on me.

'Not that I want to get away from you, I just wish things could be different. That this could all be for real. That I could come out to the world about you.

Even when we're not together, you're always there in the background, your sexy ghostly presence driving me crazy the whole time.'

'My sexy ghostly presence? Hey, I like that. I like that a lot.'

I gave him a disdainful look. Despite his annoying habits, Jimmy was the most wonderful person I'd ever met and, regardless of what he said, I knew my life would never be the same again once he'd left. No one would even come close to matching his gorgeous good looks and his funny, magnetic personality. Even George Clooney couldn't hold a candle to him. Not that George Clooney was knocking on my door, but even so. I knew I'd been spoilt for ever more.

'You know what I mean. All night long I was thinking, "Wouldn't it be nice if Jimmy was here," "Wait till I tell Jimmy this," "I wish Jimmy could try this." I wanted to share it all with you, for you to be part of it.'

'I know how hard it's been for you, Alice. You've dealt with this all so well. I'm sure most people in your situation wouldn't have kept it together for so long. It's only to be expected that things have finally got on top of you.' He pulled me to his side and we sat there in silence for a few minutes, both sipping on our tea. 'But to be honest, I'm not going to be around here for much longer. Things will get easier for you, I promise.'

'I'm not sure I want them to, not if that means losing you.' I grabbed his arm, feeling a sudden stab of fear. How could he say that? Things would be so much more difficult without Jimmy at my side. I felt a rush of heat travel up my chest, panic stirring my whole body. 'Have you heard, then? When are you going, do you know? Have you got your leaving date yet?'

He laughed.

'Whoa, whoa, slow down. I don't think it quite happens like that. No, it's just a feeling I have, Alice, but I think the time must be pretty near. There's nothing left for me to do here. I found you, Alice, and that's what this has all been about.'

'Great. And now you've found me and completely turned my world upside down you're going to drop me from a great height and leave me stranded, all alone in the world again.'

Jimmy winced. 'Don't be like that. Would you have preferred it if we'd never met?'

'No, of course not,' I said, feeling chastised. 'But how will I ever manage without you?' I folded my arms crossly, feeling like a petulant schoolgirl. 'This flat is going to be so empty and quiet without you. And how will I ever go on and have a proper relationship? With a proper man? Life will never be the same again.'

'It will. I promise you. Although that might mean a relationship with an improper man, like me. But hey, that won't be too bad, will it?' He fell silent, his gaze fixed on the daisy pattern on the duvet. 'What we've had, what we mean to each other, that doesn't change. It's for all eternity, darling.' I turned away, not wanting the tears to start again.

'You'll always be the one and only for me, Alice. But you have the whole of the rest of your life to live through and, for my sake, you need to make the most of it. After all, you'll always have the memories of our time together.' His eyes gazed at me imploringly. 'You can't spend the rest of your life mourning for the future we might have had. You need to live your life in the here and now and to the full.' He took hold of my hand, kissing my finger-tips. 'I don't want to leave you worrying about how you'll manage. You owe it to yourself and to me to live the happiest, most fulfilling life you can.'

I wasn't sure that was possible without him at my side, but I didn't want to let him down. I had to be strong.

'Of course I'll be fine,' I said, sounding more in control than I felt. 'I'm just being selfish. I've got so used to you being around. Looking after me. I can't imagine life without you now. But I'll get used to the idea. I mean, I coped well enough before you arrived, didn't I?'

I thought back to last night, the time I'd spent with Damon. People lived normal happy lives all over the place. Surely I could do the same.

'Maybe I should think about getting a cat when you're gone,' I said randomly.

Jimmy dropped his head to one side and gave me a quizzical look.

'Great. You're going to replace me with a cat?'

I laughed at his crestfallen expression.

'Well, it's a start, isn't it?'

'That's not really what I had in mind when I

said you needed to live your life to the full. You need to get out there. Meet a few people. Make some new friends. Who knows, you might even find someone special out there. Someone to spend the rest of your life with.'

How could he possibly say that?

'Well, obviously not The One because I'm The One, but there could be The Other One out there.' A mischievous smile hovered around his lips. 'Or the Next Best One. People have this misguided idea that there's only one person out there for each of us, but it's simply not true.'

'Do you think?'

'I know, Alice. Trust me. I'm not of this world. I have special insight and powers.' His hands roamed beneath the duvet and found my hipbones, his fingers tickling my tummy, making me writhe from side to side.

'Would you stop it,' I squealed.

I was laughing, but it felt like my insides were dying. I knew with an absolute certainty that I would never meet anyone to take Jimmy's place. I was destined for a life spent mourning for a man I'd never even had a proper relationship with.

'Will you promise me one thing?' I asked, suddenly serious.

'What?'

'That when it's time for you to go, you'll come and say goodbye properly. You won't just leave without telling me, will you? It's the one thing I dread.'

'Of course I won't. I've already told you that. How could you think such a thing? I wasn't planning on having a leaving party with balloons and streamers, but there's no way I'd walk off into the distance without saying a very special goodbye to my favourite girl.'

A lump appeared in my throat and I shrugged, smiling ruefully.

'Thanks, Jimmy, that's such a relief to know.'

'I have something to ask you too,' he said.

'What is it?'

'Now can I kiss you?' he said impatiently.

'Oh, yes, please,' I sighed, falling into his arms.

* * *

We were living on borrowed time, I knew that. At any moment, the lightning flash would strike between us, sending Jimmy on to his rightful place and leaving me alone in my own little world. I didn't want to think about it. For the time being, I just wanted to spend every available moment alone with him. I stepped out of the shower and was splashing my face with cold water from the sink in an attempt to get rid of the Miss Piggy look, while Jimmy brewed up some coffee in the kitchen, when my phone rang.

'Hello, Alice, it's Donna here. I hope you don't mind me calling you on the weekend.'

'Hi, Donna.' I said her name very loudly in Jimmy's direction, hoping that he hadn't been up to any of his old antics. 'No, that's absolutely fine. How are you?'

'Much better now than when I last saw you. I think I've finally hit the blooming stage, thank goodness. I'm feeling great, really happy.'

'That's good to hear.' Donna's infectious enthusiasm sang down the line.

'I was just ringing to thank you,' she hesitated, 'for sorting my, um, little problem. I don't know what it was you did, but when I got home from seeing you that day, I knew instantly that the problem had gone.'

I couldn't help the smile from spreading across my face as I wandered out from the bathroom and looked over at the 'problem', who was currently peering into my bread bin.

'Really? That's brilliant to know. I'm sure you won't have any further problems in that direction,' I said, raising my eyebrows at Jimmy.

'It's such a relief, I can't tell you. And I've learnt my lesson. I'll definitely not go round spreading nasty rumours about dead people again. Out of interest, I'd love to know, what did you do exactly to get rid of the evil spirits?'

Evil spirits? More like a mischievous, interfering and frankly too sexy for his own good spirit!

'Well,' I coughed, clearing my throat. 'I'm not supposed to divulge my secrets because then I might lose my powers, but...' I ran my hand through the bowl of potpourri on the table. 'I used a combination of special ingredients: rose petals, pine cones and, um, crystals,' I said, with what I thought was a flash of inspiration. 'Then I chanted a special spirit exorcising mantra...'

'Have you no shame?' Jimmy was shaking his head in disbelief.

'...and that usually does the trick,' I went on in my best Mystic Meg voice.

'Wow, that's amazing. You're amazing, Alice. You should be on TV with your own show. Everyone's fascinated by all that stuff.'

'Hmmm, that's an idea,' I said, stifling a giggle.

'I can't thank you enough for everything you've done for me.'

'It's an absolute pleasure, Donna. I'm just pleased that everything's worked out well for you.'

'Yes, it has,' she said, sighing happily. 'Just so as you know, the article about our engagement, the baby, the whole story is going to be in next week's magazine, so make sure you pick up a copy, won't you?'

'I will. I'll look forward to seeing it.' And for Rosemary and Michael's sake, I was relieved that they would soon have some closure on the whole sorry saga too.

26

'You'll have to get a bit more organised on the domestic goddess front once I go, Alice, you do know that? There is absolutely nothing to eat or drink in this flat bar a mouldy wedge of cheese and a bottle of champagne.'

'Ah yes, the essential supplies for any single girl about town. So breakfast is looking a bit bleak, then? Um, we could pop into town and have an early lunch or something. Then whizz round the supermarket after.'

'Hmmm.' Jimmy looked out the window, tilting his head up to study the sky. 'It's looking pretty grey out there and the forecast is heavy showers. I was thinking more along the lines of a duvet day with some good box sets and a few rounds of sand-wiches, crisps and chocolates. How does that sound?'

I sighed happily. 'Like the perfect day to me.'

'I'll pop round to the corner shop, then. Won't take me a minute. You decide on what we'll watch first and I'll be back in a jiffy.'

'Great,' I said, relieved that I wouldn't have to change out of my dressing gown after all. The only job I had to do was plump up the cushions and re-serve our places on the sofa. 'Don't be long,' I called after him.

I was certain I heard him leave, whoosh out of the front door like he always did, but moments later, I found him standing in the hallway, looking at me as if he might have forgotten something.

'Alice,' he said, walking towards me and taking me in his arms. 'You do know that I love you, don't you?'

I laughed. 'Yes, of course, what's brought all this on?'

'I just wanted to make sure.'

'Oh, you daft thing,' I chided, pushing his chest playfully. 'And I love you too.'

'Well, that's okay then. I just wanted you to know.'

'Good. So now we know where we stand, are you going out to get breakfast?'

'Ha ha, yes, of course. That's what I was doing, wasn't I?' He bent his head down, placing his lips on mine, our mouths parting together. 'I won't be long,' he said, pulling away. And then he was gone.

* * *

Some people go a whole lifetime without meeting someone special, without experiencing true love, without feeling the completeness of finding that other person who makes you feel whole. And what-ever happened now, I knew I'd been lucky enough to have experienced all those things, however fleeting they might turn out to be.

As I stood at the window, watching Jimmy's dis-tinctive outline saunter down the road, I contem-plated these things. There was no point in focusing on the negative because it was completely out of my control. So why worry?

As Jimmy said, we had to focus on the here and now. I sighed happily, placing my palms up against the window. And here and now, I was waiting for him to get to the corner at the top of the road because that's where he always stopped, turning around to look at me, giving a cheery wave in my direction. It was one of the routines we'd fallen into when Jimmy went to the 'corner shop'. Not that there was a shop on that particular corner, but he always went that way when going out for groceries, disappearing around the corner, returning with brown paper bags brimming with goodies, but I never did find out where exactly the magical corner shop was. I smiled, thinking how completely baffling it was that no one else could spot his tall, handsome, distinctly recognisable figure as he sauntered down that road.

Today, though, as he approached the corner, an uneasy feeling crept over me and my eyes stayed fixed on his back, willing him to turn around to look at me.

'Jimmy!' I urged. 'Look at me,' I cried silently.

But something told me he wouldn't look back. He kept right on walking, purposefully, determinedly. One moment, he was in my sight, and the next, he'd disappeared around the corner out of view without so much as a backwards glance.

'Jimmy!' I screamed this time, banging my fists on the window.

How could he? Why hadn't he turned round? He always did. And hadn't he promised that he wouldn't just walk away without saying goodbye? Something told me, urgently, insistently, in that moment when his unkempt black mop of hair disappeared around the corner that he'd walked out of my life for good. That was why he'd hesitated before he left, telling me he loved me. He'd been saying goodbye.

I tore off my dressing gown, letting it drop to the floor, and dashed to the bedroom, picking up the first thing that came to hand; a grubby pair of old tracksuit bottoms and a faded grey T-shirt. Hurriedly, I pulled them on, my heart beating in double-quick time, heat rushing to the extremities of my body. I wouldn't let Jimmy go. Not like this. Not without saying a special goodbye.

I slammed the door shut and ran down the stairs, taking them two at a time before flying out the front door. Tears were flowing down my cheeks as I gasped for breath.

'Jimmy!' I called. 'Please wait. Don't go. Not like this.'

I ran to the bottom of the road, stopping at the corner where I'd last seen him, looking first one way and then the other.

'Jimmy!' I repeated his name over and over again. He had to hear me. He always did. Coming running whenever I called his name.

'Are you all right, love?' A concerned old man carrying his Sunday morning paper rested his hand on my arm.

'It's my boyfriend,' I stuttered, the words accompanied by sobs. 'I've lost him.'

'Oh, don't you worry about that,' said the man, patting my arm. 'A pretty lass like you? He'd be a fool not to come back. Men? Pah. You know what we're like. You go back home, love. Mark my words, he'll be back before you know it.'

'No, not this time, he won't,' I stuttered, my gaze searching up and down the street.

'Ah, he's done this before, has he? Well, it's not for me to say, love, but if he's that type, then maybe you'll be better off without him.'

'No!' I chastised him rather too firmly. 'I have to find him. I have to. It's a matter of life and death. Jimmy,' I called, running off down the street, leaving the old man staring after me worriedly. 'Thanks.' I waved. 'And sorry,' I mouthed as I looked back, picking up speed, feeling a momentary pang of guilt.

The streets were beginning to get busy with dog-walkers, young parents pushing buggies out for an early morning stroll, people visiting the local shops for a paper and some milk. All those faces going about their daily business, seemingly without a care in the world, while the entire guts of my life were being wrenched from me, disappearing down a side street, changing my world forever.

I dashed across the road.

'Jimmy!' I hollered, cupping my hands around my mouth.

In the distance, I saw a figure striding out, the flash of blue of his top matching Jimmy's, the hair, indistinctly messy from the back, just like Jimmy's.

My heart soared. I ran after him, dodging a car and jumping onto the pavement on the other side of the road. It would be okay. I could reach him. Looking up as I headed up the street, I saw the look of terror on a lad's face as he sat astride his push-bike, freewheeling down the hill, noticed his empty satchel slung over his neck flying behind him, watched as he jammed on his brakes and as his face formed a contorted expression.

'Look out!' he cried.

But I could do nothing to stop him. Momentarily, I braced myself as the bike slammed into me, the boy catapulting off, the wheels of the bike spinning wildly as it landed on top of me, pinning me to the ground.

'Jimmy!' I mumbled helplessly.

And then everything went black.

27

'Lexie, would you do me a favour? Would you telephone work and let them know I won't be in for a while.'

'Damon, how lovely to see you. I wanted to talk to you about... hmmm, what was it exactly? I can't quite remember at the moment. Ah, well, I'm sure it will come rushing back to me. Now, would you mind popping round to the flat and checking the front door? I left in a bit of a rush and think I may have left it open.'

Silence. Nothing but a deathly silence.

Oh, well, that's charming. Just ignore me, then.

Talk amongst yourselves, why don't you? I tried again.

'Hellooo. Can anybody hear me?' God, this was so frustrating. I had so much to organise, and everyone was mooning about like a limp lettuce leaf at the end of a summer garden party. What was it with these people? And why all the long faces? Honestly, you would have thought someone had died or something, judging by all the long expressions.

'What was she doing?' Lexie's voice was faint, barely recognisable. She looked so tired and washed-out too. 'I can't understand it,' she went on. 'She never goes out without her hair done. And those old trackie bottoms, it's just not like her.'

'Maybe she'd taken up running or something.'

'You have to be kidding. She's not really the outdoors type.' She dabbed her eyes with a tissue. 'She will be all right, won't she?'

Damon took hold of Lexie's hand and squeezed it gently, nodding his head reassuringly.

'Of course she will. We need to stay positive. I just wish...' He bit on his lip, tears gathering in his eyes.

'Don't, not now.' Lexie stroked his arm, offering soothing words of comfort. 'It will be okay. It has to be okay.'

This was all very weird. Why were these two suddenly getting touchy-feely with each other? It just didn't make sense. And who exactly was that pitiful wan creature lying on the bed with tubes and monitors strapped to every conceivable part of her body?

I zoomed in on the figure of the bed and then zoomed straight back out again. Good grief. Yes, that would explain everything. It was me. Making an exhibition of myself. The room and its contents whirled around me, the bed, me lying on it, Lexie and Damon huddled together in support and all the beeping and flashing hospital paraphernalia.

How very weird. What was I supposed to do now? I couldn't hang around here in the deepest recesses of the ceiling like a wayward soul forever.

'Alice,' I heard the sing-song voice calling from behind me.

Oh, thank goodness.

'Jimmy! There you are!' Even in my discombob-ulated state, I could feel the relief seep through my body. I couldn't believe it, there he was, waiting for me, looking like he always did, only, uh-oh, much more bad-tempered. He stood beside me, arms folded, waggling a finger crossly.

'What on earth did you think you were doing, Alice?' There was a plaintive tone to his voice that tugged at my heart.

'Um... what do you mean?' My mouth and brain were having trouble working together.

It was all very confusing. What were we all doing here? Wafting around like extras on a Merchant Ivory set. Mish. Mash. Mush. The events slowly unfurled in my mind. Jimmy leaving. Me running after him. The crash.

'You left me,' I said accusingly. My head felt like the lightest whipped vanilla mousse, all frothy and full of air.

'What?'

'You left me. I watched you go and then,' it sounded ridiculous, I knew, 'you didn't wave when you got to the corner.' I paused, my head still spinning with all sorts of thoughts. 'You always waved at the corner.'

'For goodness' sake, Alice. I forgot, that was all.'

'You forgot? Oh. But then I called you and you didn't come. You always come when I call.'

'Yes, well, I didn't like to say anything, but these last few weeks, I've been losing my touch with that sort of thing.' He shrugged ruefully. 'I think my powers have been deserting me.'

'Really? So you didn't hear me, then?'

'No, I didn't hear you, Alice. I was going out for some breakfast: eggs, bacon, mushrooms, tomatoes and hash browns. I can't tell you how much I was looking forward to it, a big fry up, spending the day with you and then, well, it didn't happen, did it? You put paid to that.' He shook his head, smiling wryly. 'You are a daft thing, Alice Fletcher, do you know that? You need to be more careful out there. You could have...'

'Oh, good grief,' I shouted as more images assaulted my mind. 'That poor boy. The one on the bike. Is he okay?' His horrified face as he ploughed into me flashed into my mind.

'He's fine. Don't worry. I've been over to see him. He's collected a rather impressive number of cuts and bruises, but I have to say he came off a lot better than you. He's back at home now.'

'Thank goodness for that.' I peered down at Lexie and Damon, becoming slightly irritated now by their presence and the muffled sobs. 'Come on,' I said, turning to Jimmy, 'let's get out of here. We'll go home now and have that breakfast.'

'No, I can't, Alice.' He paused, looking serious. 'It's all over. It's time for me to go now.'

'W-what?'

'This is it, Alice.' He smiled at me beatifically, holding out his hand to me, our fingertips gently grazing.

'Oh, yes,' I cried, suddenly understanding. 'Well, this is the perfect solution, isn't it? We can be together forever, after all. I'm coming with you, Jimmy, I'm coming with you.' I could see the way, the call of the light beyond him, beckoning us both on our way.

'No, Alice, you don't understand. I have to leave. I want to go now. There's no place for me down there any more. But you, you belong there, with the people who love you. Look at them. You have to go back and live your life. It isn't your time yet.'

Tears filled my eyes.

'But I don't want to,' I said, reaching out for Jimmy's fingertips as he pulled away from me. 'I want to be with you.'

'Remember,' said Jimmy, banging his fist against his heart. 'You'll always have a place here and me with you, yeah? I love you, Alice Fletcher. And I'll be waiting for you. But that's not for now. That's way into the future. But remember your promise to me. You have to go back and live a full and happy life. Until it's your time. Damon and Lexie are waiting for you.'

No, I screamed silently inside, my scream resonating with the one currently belting from Lexie's mouth. I glared at her impatiently. My sister certainly knew how to pick her moments. Fancy having a temper tantrum now?

Lights flashed, bleepers beeped and buzzers buzzed. Nurses piled into the room, ushering Damon and Lexie outside, their anxious faces looking behind at the figure lying on the bed.

'You can't come with me, Alice, I'm sorry.'

'Please, Jimmy, take me with you. You can't leave me! Please! I'm begging you.'

'It'll be okay, Alice, I promise.' His hand swept around my head and down the side of my face, a warmth and reassurance flooding my body like a thousand rays of sunshine.

'I love you, Alice Fletcher.'

'I love you too, Jimmy.' The tears brimming in my eyes were washed away by the love and hope filling the room.

He walked backwards into the light, our fingertips reaching out to each other until the very last moment and then, as simply as he'd come into my life, he was gone.

28

'You can't go now, you've been here all this time. She'll want to see you.'

'No, I'm not so sure she will,' said Damon, pushing back his chair from the side of the bed. 'Besides, you need to spend some time alone together. Just send her my best wishes and, um, let her know I'm glad she's on the mend.'

The sound of warm, familiar voices melted over me like a chocolate fountain. Relief, that's what I felt. An overwhelming sense of comfort that everything was going to be all right. 'Jimmy,' I said to myself, as if trying the name out for the first time. I allowed myself a little chuckle. He wouldn't be coming back now, I knew that. There was a sense of completion, a finality that was strangely reassuring, and I felt only a sense of joy that I'd had the pleasure of knowing him.

'Hi, Damon.' My voice sounded weak and strange, like it belonged to someone else. I shifted in my bed and opened my eyes to look up at him.

'Hey there. How are you?' His face lit up and then he grimaced. 'Stupid question, eh?'

'I'm okay,' I said, smiling weakly. 'A bit sore.' I put my hand to my chest.

'That would be the cracked ribs, a broken wrist, concussion, cuts and bruises. Not bad for an early morning stroll.'

I laughed, then stopped abruptly, the pain getting in the way.

'Did I really do all that damage?'

Damon nodded his head sadly before he went on. 'I was just leaving, actually,' he said, gesturing towards the door.

'But do you have to?'

'Well, no... but I thought...'

'Please don't go, Damon.' My voice was strained, desperation colouring my words. 'I'd really like you to stay, if you can.' Suddenly I felt wobbly, tears gathering in my eyes as I looked from him to Lexie. I couldn't bear it if he left.

He took hold of my hand, squeezing it gently, and his touch brought a warm glow to my heart. 'Hey, I won't go anywhere if you don't want me to.'

'Do you know,' said Lexie, edging forward in her chair and taking my other hand, 'he's been worried sick. Well, we both have, but Damon hasn't left your side since we found out the news. You gave us a real scare, Alice. For a moment we thought...' Her voice trailed away as tears ran down her cheeks. 'Well, just don't ever do that to us again, will you?'

'Ha. No. I don't intend doing that again in a hurry.' I paused as I attempted to shift myself up the bed. Every movement sent arrows of pain shooting through my body. 'The boy, he is okay, isn't he?'

'Yes, don't worry, he's absolutely fine. I think his bike is in a pretty poor way, though, but Damon has been round to visit him and his parents and they're just relieved that he escaped relatively unscathed. I mean, really, he shouldn't have been cycling on the pavement and I suppose you should have been looking where you were going.' Lexie shook her head, tut-tutting. 'So it was six of one and half a dozen of the other.'

I smiled to myself, thinking of Jimmy and Damon, both taking it upon themselves to visit the lad, imagining them, two good men, bumping into each other as they did their good deed for the day.

'You did that for me?' I said, turning to Damon.

'Well, I knew you'd be worried.'

'Not only did he go and see him, but he also took him round a brand-new bike. The boy was over the moon, apparently.'

'Really?' I said, overwhelmed by his kindness. 'I feel so guilty for all the trouble I've caused. I'll make it up to you, I promise.'

'You've no need to. All you need to worry about is getting yourself better. So we can get you home and back on your feet. That's Dr Damon's orders,' he said, shaking a finger at me.

'Thank you,' I said, tears brimming in my eyes. Weariness washed over me.

He brushed the back of his hand across my cheek, before topping up the glass on the side cabinet with some fresh orange barley from a jug. 'I don't know about you, Lexie, but I could do with a coffee. Do you fancy one?'

'Ooh, yes, please,' said Lexie, giving him the thumbs up as he left the room, leaving Lexie and me alone together. As soon as he'd gone, she leant over the bed, wrapping her arms, very carefully, around me.

'I'm so glad you're going to be okay. The thought of something happening to you, well, it was just awful, really scary. Damon's been absolutely brilliant, you know. He's been such a support.'

'I know,' I said, nodding, feeling guilty at my earlier mistreatment of him. 'Hopefully things will get back to some sort of normality now.' I paused, trying to make sense of these latest events. 'Jimmy's gone now. Did you know?'

'No? Really! Well, that's good, isn't it? Sad, but good. When did he go?' I pretended not to notice the undisguised look of delight spreading across her face.

'Just... just now... I think.' Or was it an hour ago, two hours ago or even a day ago? Time had taken on an intangible quality. 'That's why I had the accident. I was running after Jimmy. I thought he was leaving me but...' I shrugged, emitting a small laugh '...I got that wrong. And then he was here with me, telling me he had to go and that my place was down here with my friends and family.'

'That's right,' said Lexie squeezing my hand tight. 'We are all here for you. So.' She paused, choosing her words carefully. 'Do you think he's gone for good, then?'

'Yes,' I nodded, 'it's all over. He's gone for good now.'

'And how do you feel about that?'

My eyes closed and I took a deep breath, conjuring up a picture of Jimmy's face in my mind.

'It's fine. Honestly, it's okay,' I said, my chest tugging at his memory. 'I'm going to miss that man so much, but it's weird, when he was here, the thought of him leaving was almost too much to bear, but when it happened, it was like it was absolutely the right thing, at the right time. Sort of natural. I don't know if that makes any sense? All I know is that it feels ...' I stopped, considering how it did actually feel. 'Good, it feels good. Like a weight has been lifted. And knowing that Jimmy is where he should be is the best thing of all. I'll never forget him.'

How could I ever forget Jimmy and everything he'd come to mean to me?

'He was like this huge ball of mischievous energy that barged into my life and turned everything upside down. And I think maybe that's why he was sent to me, to teach me something special,' I told Lexie. 'Mainly how to knock up a mean omelette, but also how to love and be loved and that's the thing that will never ever leave me.' As Lexie sat on my bed, hanging onto my every word, I saw the tears in her eyes.

I looked around the room, taking in for the first time the jugs of flowers, the helium balloons and the dozens of 'get well' cards adorning the surfaces. I felt a huge surge of gratitude, knowing I had everything to live for.

Lexie nodded, biting on her lip to stop the tears from falling.

'So no more spooky goings-on *chez toi*?'

'I guess not,' I said with a shrug.

'Everything will be okay, you do know that, don't you?' said Lexie.

'Yes,' I said, smiling, just as Damon came back through the door, bearing a tray full of coffees and biscuits. 'I'm certain everything will be okay.'

29

'It's only me!' The now familiar daily call brought a smile to my face and, something else I'd noticed these last few days, a lift to my heart. I shifted up on my elbow, the sharp pain shooting beneath my ribs a painful reminder that any movement was a bad move. I quickly sank back down again.

'Hi,' I called. 'How was your day?' Damon, his broad frame partly hidden by a huge wicker basket overflowing with potatoes, courgettes and strawberries, came into the living room.

'Productive. There's a few bits and pieces for you here. I'll just pop them in the kitchen, shall I?'

Every day since the accident, he'd made a point

of popping in on his way to work, bringing me magazines and a freshly baked brioche from the deli on
the corner, leaving me with a strict set of instructions on what I could and couldn't do, and then
calling in on his way home again.

'Remember, if there's anything you need during
the day, just ring me. I can be here in under ten
minutes.'

'Thanks, but I'll be fine,' I said smiling. Lying on
the sofa all day watching Phil and Holly, *Bargain
Hunt* and repeats of *Midsomer Murders* was hardly
very taxing. Enjoyable and worryingly addictive,
but not taxing. 'Really, there's no need to worry.'

'Hmm, but I do. Remember what the doctors
said, Alice. Don't overdo it. There's nothing you
need to do here. Just concentrate on getting yourself better. Any cleaning or ironing I can do later.'

'I'm not an invalid, you know,' I said, wincing as
I rearranged my pillows, realising I had little intention of doing either of those things anytime soon.

His doubtful look told me he thought I was exactly that.

'Dr Damon's orders,' he said sternly, pointing a
finger at me.

'Look, Damon, you know I'm very grateful for everything you've done. You've been so sweet and really helpful, but I don't want you thinking you have to come and see me every day. I'm sure you must have...'

He turned sharply to look at me.

'Do you not want me to come? Am I making a nuisance of myself? Is that it?'

'No, of course not. I look forward to you coming, but I don't want you feeling obliged or anything.'

'I don't feel obliged. Or anything,' he said, firmly.

He plonked himself down in what I'd once thought of as Jimmy's chair.

'That's okay then,' I said sheepishly. 'It's meant a lot to me just knowing that you'll be coming round, it's given me something to look forward to each day.'

'Well, that was very much the intention,' he said, looking pleased with himself. 'Oh, by the way, you had a delivery,' Damon said, suddenly remembering and jumping out of his seat. 'I meant to bring it through, but I had my arms full.'

He returned a few moments later with a cardboard box with carry handles. We shared a look together. Damon shrugged his shoulders and, intrigued, I opened the box up carefully, peering inside.

'Oh, my goodness, look what we have here. Aren't you beautiful?' A white kitten with the bluest of blue eyes stared back at me before emitting a small meow.

'A cat? Wow! Who on earth would send you a cat?'

'I don't know,' I said, transfixed by the little creature. 'I've always wanted a cat, though.' I held the kitten up to my face, feeling the softness of its fur against my skin. I bent down and tore off the tag attached to the box.

Here's a little stray who's lost his way.

And knowing how good you are with wayward souls

I thought you two would be good together.

Look after him, Alice, and he'll be sure to look after you.

Love Always xxx JM xxx

Damon took the tag from my hands and examined it. 'JM?' he asked, quizzically.

'Um...' Emotion caught in my throat. 'An old friend. He's moved away now. To a different place. The other side of the world. I won't be seeing him again, but... um... this must be his leaving gift. What a lovely gesture, don't you think?' I said, beaming, tears rolling down my cheeks.

'Er, yes, I guess,' he said, looking totally bemused. 'If you're absolutely sure it's what you want. What are you going to call it?'

'I don't know,' I said, staring into the kitten's curious eyes. 'He's so sweet, isn't he?' I tickled the skin beneath his chin. 'Like an angel sent down from heaven.'

Damon shook his head, laughing.

'Angel it is, then,' he said, cradling the cat gently in his arms. 'Come on, Angel, let's show you round your new home, mate.'

Sometimes you have a feeling about things, a gut instinct, and every instinct in my body told me everything would work out okay after all.

ACKNOWLEDGMENTS

It's been a pleasure revisiting this story and reacquainting myself with one of my very favourite heroes, Jimmy Mack. I must admit to being more than just a little in love with him.

Thanks to everyone who made this book possible, my long-standing writing group, my ever-supportive family and friends, and to the editors who have worked with me on this story to bring it to this final finished version. Special thanks to the entire Boldwood team for giving me the opportunity to bring this book to a whole new audience.

Finally, thanks to you, my lovely reader, for selecting my book from all those other amazing books out there. I really hope you enjoy the read.

MORE FROM JILL STEEPLES

We hope you enjoyed reading *When We Meet Again*. If you did, please leave a review.

If you'd like to gift a copy, this book is also available as an ebook, digital audio download and audiobook CD.

Sign up to Jill Steeples' mailing list for news, competitions and updates on future books.

https://bit.ly/JillSteeplesNews

Starting Over at Primrose Woods, another uplifting story from Jill Steeples, is available now.

ABOUT THE AUTHOR

Jill Steeples is the author of many successful women's fiction titles – most recently the Dog and Duck series - all set in the close communities of picturesque English villages. She lives in Bedfordshire.

Visit Jill Steeples's website: https://www.jillsteeples. co.uk

Follow Jill on social media:

 twitter.com/jillesteeples
 facebook.com/jillsteepleswriter

ABOUT BOLDWOOD BOOKS

Boldwood Books is a fiction publishing company seeking out the best stories from around the world.

Find out more at www.boldwoodbooks.com

Sign up to the Book and Tonic newsletter for news, offers and competitions from Boldwood Books!

http://www.bit.ly/bookandtonic

We'd love to hear from you, follow us on social media:

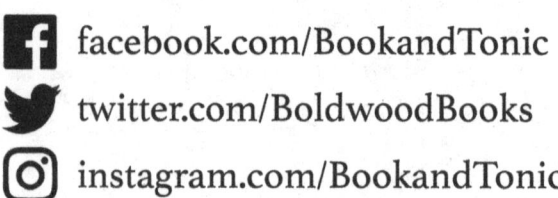

facebook.com/BookandTonic

twitter.com/BoldwoodBooks

instagram.com/BookandTonic